godless children have no heroes

LBAkles

Print version: ISBN 978-1-7368045-0-6

ebook version: ISBN 978-1-7368045-1-3

Book Design by HMDpublishing

Acknowledgements

I am grateful for my life, for the support and opportunity to express my creativity and speak freely:

For Michael and Holly Lee, who didn't make it. For Susie who did. For Carrie. For my family...the one that made me and the one that I made. For those who tried their best. For those who did their best. For Sarah and Kimmy. For JoAnne who really made a difference. For Susan, who I love and who loves me. For my amazing children Samantha, Madison and Katelyn who I hope feel safe and loved.

For godless children everywhere. I hope you find a place.

This story is fiction and some of it is true...

godless: the state of having no stable, secure influence to build the core self, leaving the individual without guidance; to build an empty, unstructured, chaotic, and self-determined sense of self, based on nothing; lost...

Prologue

'Reckless'

Tires squealed as the dark gray SUV took the freeway off ramp too quickly.

The speakers blared.

"I can feel my heart beat out my chest, you know that I would die for this..."

Sixty...seventy...eighty miles per hour.

Lex kept her eyes straight ahead, not daring to look at the image raging in the rear view: the white sports car was still just a touch from her rear bumper. Ahead, an intersection.

"Please," she pleaded out loud, sucking in her breath.

She closed her eyes, barreled through...and nothing. She sighed in relief only a moment. The pursuing vehicle bumped her slightly. Both hands gripped the steering wheel instinctively, her right hand releasing quickly at the sharp pain shooting through her right wrist and swelling hand.

"Stupid, stupid, stupid. You are so screwed," she muttered.

The realization loomed heavy that she was never going to outrun a sports car. She cursed herself for her vehicle choice.

'...don't call me out 'cause I let you down...'

The car hit again. She hadn't considered that this would be how she would die. She hadn't considered that she would have so much time to think about it when it came. And what if she survived anyway? Nothing would be normal again, not that it was normal now, but how could she ever talk her way out of a fate that would be worse than death: life in a cell. So, this was how it would end.

She just hoped it would be quick.

"Fuck!" she said under her breath, resigned.

She hit the brakes hard.

The sports car swerved in reaction but clipped the back of her vehicle, sending the car flying over, landing on its top and skidding down an embankment where it tumbled, only stopping at the bottom. The force of the hit sent the SUV into a violent spin, crashing finally into a wall.

Only others bore witness to this: The force of the initial hit popped the side airbags open where her head hit, knocking her unconscious.

"...and I will do whatever it takes, I'm still hungry..."
-Adelita's Way

'Reckless...'

Before...

1

Their world was perfect. A normal life. A wonderfully safe boring life. In the middle of a world in chaos, they thrived. Life, career, family, pets, vacations. Lilah was an executive project lead at a biomedical company, Lex a software developer working for a security research group. Where Lilah was outspoken and charismatic, Lex was quiet, though not shy, with an opinion. Their son, Aiden, was completing his surgical residency. He had married young, too young, in their shared opinion, but the girl made him happy, and whatever hesitation they had in the beginning was long forgotten once their granddaughter was born: beautiful little Avery who was the love of all of their lives.

Their world was perfect. Until it wasn't. Until Lilah felt some swelling in her neck, went for a checkup, and was diagnosed with Anaplastic Thyroid Cancer. Instantly, unimaginably, their lives changed.

"Unfortunately, ATC is extremely aggressive," the doctor told them quietly.

He was an intruder, this sterile man sitting behind an oversized desk in a sterile office delivering this well-rehearsed death sentence much too easily, and though he spoke slowly and clearly, Lex barely heard the words. As he continued, she heard only the low hum building in her ears as they grew hot. It felt to her that her heart was pounding so hard that it was causing her brain to knock against her skull.

Lilah was calm as she listened to this prognosis, to the less than one year survival rate. The room held a dark silence. That small unbelievable speech knocked the wind out of her. She glanced quickly at Lex. The pale silent woman looking back made her suck in her breath even more: this was real. How this happened or why seemed a cruel, unanswerable question that bound her chest like a life vest pulled too tight, stealing life's breath instead of saving it.

"What do we do?" Lilah heard herself say finally.

"The treatment is mostly palliative," the physician stated frankly.

"What does that mean?" Lex demanded, not able to control her tone or the anger she began feeling for him as she switched into long forgotten survival mode.

He sighed thoughtfully before speaking. "Well, we should discuss radiation. I will try to get you into a clinical trial. There are some encouraging results..."

"...And that might extend my life, what? One, two years?" Lilah interrupted. Her words were controlled though Lex saw the shock wearing off into the pale of fear.

Her question was met with silence.

That evening as they were cuddled together on the sofa, the silence between them was, for the first time in ages, uncomfortable. Lex's heart had been ripped out, her soul crushed. She was nothing, just a numb shell, a blood pumping mechanical oxygen machine. Dead inside. Empty.

It was Lilah who broke the silence.

"It's ironic," she stated finally.

"What is?" Lex asked.

"We do clinical trials for cancer medication all the time. I'd basically be putting myself into my own study," she answered.

"That's good, right? I mean, you have the insider information on the one with the most promising results," Lex stated hopefully.

Lilah's silence told Lex everything. Who would know better what was promising?

"What do you want to do?" Lex asked her cautiously.

"It's we. What do we want to do," Lilah answered.

"We want you to do what it takes to fix you."

"Lexi..."

"I know." Lex pulled away and took a breath that she hoped would hide her irritation. "Why do you do that? Why say we when it's not? It's right for you to do what is best for you, because I want what you want, but honestly, it's not we."

"It is we, Lex," Lilah's response was quiet but definite. "We don't want life as a series of treatments and illness only to put off what is inevitable. We've talked about this so many times. Live the life we have while we can."

"Yes, but that was before any of this was reality," Lex interrupted, knowing it was futile, knowing it was selfish, because roles reversed, it would be the same.

"We're lucky, we've been happy. Aiden's grown. We have Avery," Lilah said with a small smile.

"Fine." Lex sighed, resigned.

She held her sadness, swallowed it, where it sat heavy in her stomach and tight in her chest. Later, when Lilah was in bed watching the news and Lex felt secure that the TV and running water created an adequate sound barrier, she sat in the shower sobbing, knees to her chest, as the water streamed over her. Warm steam filled her lungs, and she choked on it as her mind was now allowed to race freely with the thought of losing Lilah, of being alone, of having no control. Lex knew this alone well, understood it in a way that no one should, and though the water ran hot, a chill ran through her at the prospect of this as the sadness turned to fear.

They avoided the truth for a few days: Get up, go to work, have dinner, talk about the day. They avoided telling Aiden; this time was going to be the time, then next time. Each time they were going to see him was always going to be the time. And yet Lilah always changed her mind.

"Let him have another day to wake up in his world, not ours...not yet," she would say.

This continued for a couple weeks, and perhaps it could have lasted longer. But reality, in the form of Lilah almost passing out in front of Aiden, decided for them. And so, they sat with their son at the breakfast table where they had shared so many happy and important experiences over his lifetime: birthday surprises, college acceptance, finding out they would be grandparents. And they told him.

Aiden swallowed his shock and turned quickly into the doctor he was becoming, his questions clinical, sterile.

'So much like her,' Lex observed.

The sickness in Aiden's stomach was unlike anything he had ever experienced, what he could only describe as like having a high fever in his brain. He fought the devastating sadness silently and began to question his life as his mothers answered his questions. What point was there to being a doctor when he couldn't even save his own mother? How would he ever again be on the other side of this, telling someone they were dying, without the memory of hearing this from his parents? He didn't dare dwell on the questions and forced the thoughts away, listening but not listening, while they sat in front of him pretending to be calm and in control. He hoped his fear didn't show. The conversation was awkward, rehearsed. The paused silence between words filled with what he could only guess was the shock setting in.

On that day, as Aiden left for his shift, he gathered strength and hugged Lilah tightly. It was only when hugging Lex that he trembled, struggling to hold the sorrow. Lex squeezed him tighter to her briefly, then just as quickly let him go. If she had held on any longer, she feared she would lose any sense of emotional control. There would be time for that later. A lifetime.

"We'll talk soon," he whispered.

And it was decided: Live the life they had. And then life became something else. Something stark and matter of fact: Lilah was going to die.

Lex walked through the days numb to existence. Everything now was about Lilah: where she wanted to go, what she wanted to do, to eat, to see. This was all that mattered. Living for the moment was their day to day now, and in this, Lex struggled. She could hear herself talk and laugh. She could hold Lilah close in those horrible, tearful moments, mourning her life cut short: She wouldn't see Avery grow up, they wouldn't grow old together, and through all of it, Lex was there and would continue to be there, but she was not present, because being present would make all of it too real and unbearable. Whenever Lex contemplated life without Lilah, an uncontrollable panic would threaten to take over, and this was completely unacceptable. Panic was weak. Panic was the last thing she wanted Lilah to see.

It was at night, only at night in veiled darkness, when sleep eluded her that Lex felt truly present. In this calm silence, she would reminisce, staring at the pictures of their life, picking up and holding the little trinkets collected over the years. She would let herself smile with the memory of these items; the rocks and shells Aiden had been obsessed with collecting from different vacations, the ceramic bowl made during one of those 'go out and create' couples' activities, the revolver: a movie replica given to her by Lilah simply because she liked it.

Her fingers left a thin, clean line across the barrel as she ran her fingers over the top of it reminding her that normal activities, even her obsessive regular dusting, had ceased. It was in this dark and heavy bubble of reality that she would allow selfish tears.

As Lilah was dying, so was Lex's soul. A sharp deep darkness grew undenied. Old demons summoned and whispered uncertainty for this life, this vulnerable hopeful impossible life now becoming hopelessly impossible. How fragile and precious these years had been, to be taken away so swiftly, without mercy or negotiation. She found herself angry: with herself for allowing the vulnerability of love, and with Lilah for the promise of safety and hope that had allowed the wall she'd built early to crumble and decay. This complete exposure caused panic that was difficult to escape, and she could not rebuild the fortress quickly enough. How could Lilah be taken from her? It was completely unimaginable and still unacceptable even though every rational, logical solution to fix this had led back to the fact that this was not fixable.

It was Avery who brought that sense of joy and hope to their apocalypse. Avery, sweet, soft and pink, a beginning of endless possibility cuddled in that soft, sweet baby smell, a smile in this darkest moments of their lives.

Lex's strength, what there was of it, was only for Lilah, and for Aiden, and every other part of her slowly unraveled. She was, for the first time in decades, completely alone. The familiar terror swirling in her soul was exhausting, desperate and inescapable.

Years back, Lilah's father had been ill for quite some time before he passed away, and what Lex remembered most clearly was that the facade of daily life was just that: a little lie that everything was normal and yet even the most normal activity was overshadowed with the sense of finality. Truth mocked her: the alarm to take medication, the uncertainty of good days to bad days, the physical changes, the loss of Lilah's independence, her frustration...all stark intruders interrupting the lie.

But lie they did, to each other and to everyone else. When Lilah looked tired, it was Lex who said she needed a break. When Lilah seemed the most in pain, it was Lex who would step in:

"Babe, you think we can sit this one out? I'm not feeling it today."

When they were with friends:

"Lilah, I'm really sorry, there's a work emergency..."

Lilah would always give Lex a knowing look of gratitude. This was the way they chose to deal with 'it.' Any other discussion beyond the general, "Do you need anything? Is there a prescription to pick up?" was out of bounds once Lex asked Lilah for the thousandth time:

"How are you feeling?"

"The same as when you asked yesterday," Lilah had snapped back.

"I'm sorry, I didn't mean to upset you," Lex had replied uncomfortably.

"No. It's just...I feel like everyone stares at me like I'm going to break, it's really making me angry," Lilah had explained.

In an effort to maintain what was left of her sanity, Lex placed focus on a project that allowed her to pass the long periods of time when Lilah slept.

Writing code was absolute. It required no emotion. Code could be directed to do anything. Code could be controlled, and that was what she needed to keep going: Code couldn't die. This is how Lex survived.

On the surface, it was a child's game: little animated two-dimensional rabbits pulling carrots, some putting them into baskets, some eating them. However, with the right sequence on the game controller, a small, embedded window gave her access into the soul of the web, allowing her the ability to do anything. The core of the software was security based, something she helped develop a few years ago, another lifetime ago, it felt. 'Out of the box,' it had helped keep data safe. With the code reversed, what was once a gate was now an open door to almost anything. Instead of locking down intruders, it cleared a path for them, for her. It bounced IP addresses, scrambling them. She added a function that virtually broke apart the number sequences, with each hop, scattering them into oblivion. Built directly into a game system. Separate from their home network. No computer. Untraceable. Completely. Because she could.

In spite of the looming sadness, she had felt a rush of satisfaction that was validated with a test run that easily shut down the power on a neighborhood block. Releasing control only when hearing reports of the outage, she waited. It was innocent enough and untraceable. She had hoped. In her head, she created an explanation for the hack. She had practiced this in her head...working on an advanced security patch for work and accidentally shut off the power. But the power was restored, and the 'cause' was determined to be a random power surge.

Deep down, Lex knew this was a bad path, but she was a dying star giving in to the pull of the black hole of her life. She escalated.

"What are we doing?" Lilah inquired one evening, noticing a smile from Lex, the first genuine smile in weeks. She curled up next to her.

"We are playing a game," Lex responded and handed the game controller to Lilah.

Lilah moved a rabbit around the screen for about a minute.

"Honey, I may be missing something, or maybe it's the meds, but this looks like the most boring video game ever. I mean, what's the point?" she asked.

"Wow. Hurtful," Lex teased. "Trust me, these are busy little rabbits."

On the screen, one little animated rabbit pulled carrots from the ground and put them in a basket, and when full, another rabbit picked it up and stacked it on the back of a truck. At the same time that this played out on the screen, miles away, a city councilwoman's bank account was being emptied of a substantial amount of money and transferred to a graffiti cleanup charity, something she had promised to focus on but had yet to deliver.

Lilah handed the controller back to Lex. "Are you hacking something?" she asked. Her voice sounded serious. Or maybe worried. Lex wasn't sure.

Silence.

"Lex?" she said again.

"Lilah...it's not what you think."

'Since when do I lie to her?' Lex thought.

Lilah was thinking the same thing. "Lex, seriously."

It made sense to Lilah that this was where Lex would hide herself, and though she felt disappointed in this return to old behavior, Lilah didn't let on.

"Ok, I just want to see if this works," Lex explained, "it will be a good thing, I promise."

It was Lilah's truth that their whole life together had been honest. Lex was intelligent and talented and, once upon a time, a bit dangerous, and it had been exciting and somewhat frightening, and Lilah almost walked away. A lifetime ago...

Mazzy Star's "Fade into You" haunted her memory of that evening in Lex's Hollywood apartment when everything changed. When Lilah came home to find Lex sleeping head down at the computer in the same clothes she'd had on the day before.

There were empty soda cans everywhere around the desk, on the desk, on the computer monitor. The computer was beeping steadily. Frustrated, Lilah kicked one of the cans, causing Lex to wake up. She rubbed her eyes for a moment, and noticing the beeping said, "Oh damn," and began typing.

"How was your day, babe?" she asked without looking up, seeming oblivious that Lilah had kicked the can on purpose and also oblivious that she was angry.

Lilah stood in silence staring at the woman she had wanted to spend her life with. Now, she wasn't sure. More and more, this was the routine and less and less Lilah was a part of it.

"What are you working on this time?" she asked angrily.

Lex began to answer but stopped short of actually telling her the details, the pause indicating the realization that Lilah was angry.

"What's wrong?" she asked Lilah.

"You're what's wrong," Lilah responded.

"What does that even mean?"

"You...this," Lilah motioned to the computer.

"I don't get it," Lex stated, "what does a computer have to do with anything?"

"This is all you do, for those creepy people, all the time..."

"No, not all the time," Lex interrupted, "and not everyone is creepy. Odd maybe."

"Most of the time," Lilah shot back.

"Lilah, this is a job, it's how I pay for school, this place," Lex stated.

Lilah took a deep breath, feeling her eyes heat up with the beginnings of tears. She rubbed the hair back out of her face then responded quietly:

"It's not a job, it's hacking, manipulating, stealing." She walked over to the counter, picking up a pile of half opened mail. "These are jobs, real jobs, honest career building jobs. All of these companies want you, and you're just barely finishing your degree."

Lilah stopped, realizing that she was crying now. Lex didn't respond, she just looked at her, confused.

"Don't you get it? Anything?" Lilah choked out.

"It's the same thing," Lex responded. "Code is code, money is money."

"No Lex, it's not. These," Lilah held up the pile of mail, "these won't get you hurt or killed, these won't get you arrested. These won't make me lose you."

She was full blown crying now.

"Fuck. Forget it." She walked out of the living room.

Curled up on the edge of the bed, looking out a window that faced a brick wall, Lilah sighed deeply. She was always scared now, always worried that Lex would get hurt, always wondering if the next knock at the door would be the police, the FBI, some criminal. It was just too much. She felt Lex sit next to her on the bed.

"Lilah?" Lex said. Lilah didn't respond. "Lilah, I'm sorry."

Lilah rolled over.

"You don't even know why I'm so upset do you?"

"Not really," Lex admitted.

"Great."

"Lilah, I don't understand. This never bothered you before. I've been doing this since before I knew you. It's not like I'm lying to you."

"I know, Lex, I just...How long do you think you can really get away with this? How are we supposed to have a life, a home? Maybe this made sense before, but I want a life. Don't you?"

Watching Lex think, Lilah could read her easily...Lex thought she was having a life. And maybe this was the only life she could picture. Lex was smart enough not to say that out loud.

"Of course, I do," she responded. "Look, honestly it doesn't matter what I do or how I do it. What matters is you. Life is only life with you, Lilah. So, if it's going to make you happy, I'll stop."

"Really?" Lilah sat up. The response had been unexpected.

"Yes, really," Lex said, making an invisible cross over her heart. "Absolutely. Done. I'll fry the hard drive, I won't touch a computer again until I decide on one of those 'corporate,' blah, jobs."

Lex had chosen her over that life.

The thought of Lex crossing her heart caused Lilah to smile briefly, and yet, as she listened to Lex enthusiastically explain what she had built, Lilah couldn't escape the worry that she had, in fact, been living in a blissful delusion that somehow she had changed Lex. That their life together, their bond, their child had calmed the darkness and filled her soul with light and strength. That this replaced her obsessive need to manipulate the world around her in an effort to run from fear. That love had been enough to give her the strength to live, not just survive.

Lilah convinced herself that this was ok, that Lex needed to work through all of this and that in the end, Lex would accept her death and move on. She forced herself to have faith that their life together would give Lex the desire to live a happy life. Lilah needed to believe this.

"Lilah, are you even listening?" Lex asked.

"Huh? Oh." Lilah cuddled close to Lex, brushing off the question and laughing. "You know, I really don't follow all of this past Coding 101. So who exactly are we doing what to?"

The next day, the councilwoman could not escape the good press bombarding her office. How could she now go on record and state that someone had stolen the money? True, this was money she had skimmed bit by bit over the past year. True, the money had originally been intended for the exact project she had stolen it from. The same project she had been saying for months that the city simply had no room for in the budget. Staring out from behind the podium, she prepared herself for the announcement. To do anything else would be admitting that she had no intention of ever moving forward with funding the effort and, in fact, had only been funding herself. And this was an election year.

The councilwoman took a breath and let it out slowly. Someone knew. But who? Who could possibly know the exact amount? She convinced herself she was not in danger of being exposed because the money was now where it should have been. Still, the tightness in her chest told her something entirely different. Someone now owned her.

'Well played,' she thought as the camera crew counted down.

The councilwoman was all smiles for the cameras as she spoke, and Lex and Lilah caught the tail end of the news clip:

"...and was important to me to uphold my commitments to this community. That I meant it when I said, 'Community First.' So, I've led the way, and I think we can get there together."

Then she looked directly into the camera.

"I hope that all of you so committed to this project know that I will do whatever it takes to reach our shared goal. Let's work as a team. Visit the website ..."

Lilah found herself laughing, for the moment ignoring the worry and the long-term implications of Lex's interference.

"I hate that woman," she said out loud.

That was the beginning. Something for them to talk about completely separate from illness. Some good and some humor in all of the bad. Little things. Investments. Small untraceable justices. Lex kept it lowkey, taking leave from real work so that she could be with Lilah. It was unspoken and a given. It was a harmless video game. Cute cartoon graphics doing basic tasks. A game.

But that was before.

2

As the weeks passed and winter's early darkness brought the night sooner, Lex found herself sleeping less and only from complete exhaustion, because sleep brought the demons that were hard to escape. On rare occasions though, Lex would dream of sitting in the window of her college library. Through the window, she would watch Lilah talking to a group of people in the courtyard below; people gathered closely around her, listening and laughing as she spoke, acting so much more like an audience than a group of peers. From Lex's position, she could not hear the words being exchanged; only library conversation whispered softly in her ears.

Lilah's hands moved expressively as she spoke. There was a welcome beauty to her movements, so full of passion and energy, and it made Lex smile to observe through the opaque haze that never let her forget that she was dreaming.

On this night, after what had been a particularly bad day for Lilah, Lex found solace in this dream that allowed her Lilah to be free from the pain and constant exhaustion. The peace was interrupted by her phone.

"Mom, are you alone?" Aiden asked.

"No," she answered quietly. The tone of his voice made her face warm with worry. "Lilah's sleeping next to me. What's up?"

"Everything is ok. Avery is ok, but there was an accident..."

Lex navigated the hospital hallways in a panic, finding her way finally when she caught a glimpse of Aiden. She slowed to a steady pace, not wanting to create a scene. As she approached, she heard quiet arguing. As she got closer, the tension was palpable. Their demeanor told the truth: this was no accident.

They knew instantly that she knew.

As she approached them, Melissa looked away, wiping her tear-stained face. Aiden stepped between them.

"Where's Mom?" he asked calmly as she pulled him into an embrace.

"She's parking. You know she still insists on driving when she can," she answered.

"Mom don't. Please," he pleaded in a whisper into her ear. "Please just...Avery is safe...I didn't know...I just, give me time to figure this out."

She stepped back and stared silently at Melissa.

'I'm going to kill you,' she thought.

A feeling that Lex thought had been left behind a lifetime ago stirred in her. It was like rage and fear fighting each other, and it was hot and quick. She struggled to be rational and fought the part of her that wanted to jump on the woman in front of her and smash her head into the floor. She was angry with herself, for the docile shell of the person she was now. The old Lex would have seen this coming a mile away, that something deep in a person, something broken and cruel that could not be fixed. But now, the old self saw it clearly in her daughter-in-law's soul. She swallowed it, and through a cold sweat, she could taste the bitterness of the softball in her throat.

Aiden felt his world spinning in disbelief and helplessness. He felt like it must be shock, ironically, that was keeping him sane. First, his little girl's fingers were broken and his wife was clearly lying;

"Oh my god Aiden! Avery's hand got wedged in the side of the changing table," Melissa told him hysterically over the phone, "I picked her up and I didn't see that her hand was caught."

But the x-ray of Avery's little broken fingers was not consistent with this explanation and made this story a lie.

And Lex's reaction...Aiden could tell that she knew. He had never seen his mother look the way she did. He expected anger, or maybe tears. But the person who approached him and the expression on her face didn't reflect his mother at all. This look was calm and dark, and he admitted to himself that it scared him.

They briefly stood in silence as Lex pictured herself grabbing the crying woman by the hair, stabbing a blade through her neck and watching as she struggled to breathe, choking on the blood gushing from the open wound.

'Save your tears, you fuck, I see you now,' her brain silently narrated to this fantasy.

"Where is my granddaughter," she said calmly, her trance broken by Lilah's approach...

"Aiden!" Lilah called out and grabbed him and Melissa into an embrace. "Oh my God, what happened? Where is Avery?"

Relieved at the interruption, Melissa grabbed Lilah's hand and led her into the room. As she began to follow behind, Lex caught the expression on her son's face and realized in an instant that he must have been studying her initial reaction, the old Lex. She struggled to find the softness of the Lex that he knew and wrapped her arm through his.

"Everything will be alright," she told him quietly. This was enough to move him forward.

Much later in the hospital room, Lex sat with Avery, caressing the child's wrapped hand through the bars of the crib as she slept. For Aiden's sake, and mostly for Lilah's health, she had promised him secrecy, at least to give him a chance to figure out his next move.

"Grandma missed it Sweet Girl," she whispered to the sleeping infant. "I'm so sorry, princess. We just have to be patient now, don't we?"

Yes, there was indeed something broken, something cruel and familiar. She knew it well.

The memory of a poor, sweet little neglected dog, Peanut, flashed in her head. He was a ghost from her young life, virtually nonexistent. Where did he eat? Sleep? Did she play with him outside? Did her sister love him? The memory was fuzzy as always, just bits and pieces flashing in her brain. He might as well have been one of her many discarded toys in the toybox. But he came later, right?

Lex watched her son sleep restlessly in a chair and watched Avery's chest rise with each sleeping breath in the quiet hospital room. This other life, the memory of the dog, continued to plague her.

First, there was the little black and white Rat Terrier, in her life before her life. Her first real love that Lexi's parents had found discarded in the mud on the side of the road before she was born. Her protector who would growl and snap at her mother when Lexi was to be punished.

Lexi was six when he died, and she cried oceans of tears until finally her mother told her to stop crying. After, pets came and went. But they too disappeared as quickly as they came: one day there, and one day...

"We set them free."

Gone; sent to the imaginary farm or new home, wherever pets go when parents send them away.

Peanut had been in the back yard as they ate dinner that evening. Her mother was at work. The guttural growl of animals on the attack suddenly filled the silence. A stray dog had entered the yard, and they were teeth to neck in battle. Her stepfather grabbed a baseball bat from the garage, ran to the dogs and lifted the bat. For a moment, a very brief moment, he hesitated, and she caught his eye. It was cruel, an evil smile directed right at her. Through her. He brought the bat down, not on the stray, but on Peanut, knocking him out. Lexi froze in fear.

When her mother had asked what happened, he swore to her that he was so sorry, that he missed the stray and accidentally hit Peanut. But Lexi knew it was no accident. This was now a silent agreement between the two of them:

'I can do whatever I want,' beamed from his eyes.

Lexi was terrified.

Peanut was never the same. Neither was Lexi.

Her adult self was under that same old spell. At home the next day as Lilah slept, Lex found herself re-living the dog in a repeating loop in her head. She felt sick to her stomach and couldn't stop shaking. She headed to the living room and turned on the game console, mindlessly working.

"She said it was an accident," Aiden had stated through tears. "Mom, I don't know what to do. Do I owe her that chance? What was she thinking? How could she do this?"

He was such a kind, thoughtful young man. Even a little naive. This was Lilah and his Grandpa Al's influence, and Lex had always been grateful, always fearing he would be more like her. This, though, this had broken her child.

She listened as he struggled. How could his wife, who never even raised her voice, even when they argued, how could she be this person who lost her temper and hurt her daughter? His daughter. What was he missing? He was so confused and angry. Now, he was *that* parent, the one he had spoken with on many occasions during his Emergency Medicine rotation. The one he had often thought was lying when they said they didn't know...now he had let his child be *that* child. It was his greatest and most important responsibility, and he had failed.

Lex did her best to comfort him. How could he understand? He hadn't been raised in a turbulent home, hadn't experienced chaos or violence. They made sure of that. No training in the world could prepare him for this.

No. This would have been up to Lex to catch. And she would have, had she not let herself become... what? Whatever she was now? With Lilah? The old Lex would have been vigilant, would have dug further into her daughter-in-law's background. She would have never accepted that Melissa's relationship with her family ended when she could no longer commit to the hypocrisy of their ultra-religious rules, or her father's ongoing drug addiction. The old Lex would have seen this coming. She would have known better. This was on her. And it was on Lilah for making her promise to never use her "skills" in their personal life.

So, she waited. She was trapped. She lied her support to Melissa. For Lilah.

"You have to know, you have to believe that I am so sorry. Please believe me. I don't know what happened. I love Avery more than life," Melissa sobbed.

"We all want what's best for all of you," she said more than once, always choking back hot, razor-sharp rage. "We will get through this as a family."

This was Lex and Melissa in front of Aiden. Alone, which they were rarely, there was little to no conversation. Lex had made clear her position:

"I've made an appointment for you," Lex heard herself tell the young woman, knowing her voice was cold and blatant. "You will see this therapist. You will comply with whatever he says."

"Yes, I will. Thank you for forgiving me, for giving me this chance to prove..."

Lex cut her off, "Forgive you? This isn't mine to forgive. There's no proving, because there is no trust. You're never going to be alone with Avery for more than a little time, if ever. I will be caring for her unless her father is home. And you better not say anything to Lilah, ever."

She looked Melissa directly in the eyes, "I think that's best for everyone, right?"

Melissa could only nod.

Lex held her gaze. *'Do not push me.'*

"I'll work out Avery's schedule with Aiden, then," she commanded.

Lex didn't doubt the regret in the young woman's statement, it read in her eyes, her voice. She appeared to be a wounded child, and like a wounded child, Lex could read the defensive anger, and that said more than anything: This was a woman struggling to survive, not a woman who had made a terrible immature mistake. And for that, Lex wouldn't bring herself to care for Melissa or her well-being even the slightest. She refused to feel sorry for the young girl she must have once been or what endured trauma that could lead to this. She refused to accept or believe any sincerity Melissa expressed. No. This was a choice, pure and simple. And now, Lex was indeed the mother-in-law from Hell, and she owned it. Whatever would keep Avery safe.

They lived this lie for Lilah...that this was just an accident, in the fear that the truth would have broken her heart, and that the added worry would worsen the illness. Lex bit her tongue more than once and played 'happy family.' Aiden was vigilant. They all were. Avery was just with them more so that Lilah could spend as much time with her as possible, that was their story. Lie on top of lie leading to a continued series of lies built on more lies, but Lex didn't care. As long as Avery was safe, it was Lilah's health that was most important. Her peace and happiness were everything.

But it killed Lex that Lilah expressed her gratitude."Melissa, you are so wonderful to rearrange your life for me, so that I can have this time with Avery. I'm so grateful to you," she'd heard Lilah tell her.

This was a consequence of the lie that Lex had to live with, and Melissa played the part well, reveling in Lilah's attention. This routine was life now.

3

As the illness progressed, Lilah became obsessed with pictures: Every moment documented, every picture pointless and painful to Lex. Why create more to be sad about? But it was important to Lilah, so it was important to her, and Lilah's favorite subject was, of course, their granddaughter. Countless hours of wardrobe changes, different scenery, a day at the park.

"Here, take this picture," she'd instruct Lex, holding Avery on a swing, "Did you get it?"

"Yes."

"Ok, over here now. Wait, I want to get her hat..."

"Lilah, I think we have enough. It's chilly. You look tired, let's go home," Lex told her.

"No, I want one with her against that tree," Lilah responded, dismissing her.

It was like having an argument with a child.

"Seriously, c'mon already. She's barely even awake," Lex complained.

"No. I want her to have this one, please?" Lilah pleaded. "C'mon and get in the picture."

Lex acquiesced, "Fine, but then we are going."

Lex had very few pictures from her childhood: a couple as an infant, one of her sister, but they were only a reminder of loneliness and isolation. They had volumes of pictures of her and Lilah and Aiden through the years. As she watched Lilah pose their granddaughter, it occurred to her that she had never been the one to initiate the taking of or even asking for a picture to be taken. She admittedly enjoyed having them but now, when she looked at the happy, smiling images, they seemed only a lie as she waited in anxious anticipation for things to fall apart. Or maybe they had already.

Time passed unforgivingly, and Lilah grew weaker as the cancer advanced and the prescribed medication began to lose its effectiveness.

"Let me get you something stronger," Lex begged. "I can get you anything."

"Illegal," Lilah replied, her one-word answer meant to shut down the conversation.

"What does it matter now? If it makes you feel better..."

"No. Lex," was her response, "this isn't who you are. C'mon, just because you can doesn't mean you should."

Sensing Lex's frustration in her plea, Lilah paused. She chose her next words carefully:

"Honey, I know you feel lost and mad..."

"I'm not mad," Lex interrupted, but Lilah continued:

"I know you are mad. It's ok. I'm mad, too. This sucks. It isn't fair. But this is where we are. I need you to be there for our family. This road you're on...you know where it fucking leads. It's not who you are. That person is gone."

Lilah was wrong. This was exactly who Lex was, but arguing that fact with Lilah was futile, and upsetting her was worse than convincing her otherwise. If that's what Lilah needed to believe, then let her believe.

"You're right, Lilah," she responded quietly, "I just don't want to see you in pain."

"Promise me that you will stop now. No more game, or hacking or whatever you are doing," she pleaded. "Don't throw our life away."

"I promise," she lied with a sigh, hoping she at least sounded sincere.

And the days passed routinely.

It was on a particularly gray Saturday morning in March that Aiden finally lost it. The utter exhaustion and simmering anger of pretending had taken a toll. This wasn't him. No matter the reason, no matter the solution or help, it was not fixable. As she watched him pace around the living room, Lex thought he looked tired and disheveled and too old for his age.

Aiden had just come from what felt like the hundredth argument with Melissa:

"Are you ready to head over to Moms'?" he called to Melissa from their living room.

He heard her chatting away to Avery in the nursery. Every time she stopped talking Avery giggled in response, and he went to join them, stopping just at the doorway to watch the exchange. Melissa stood next to the crib, still in her pajama shorts and tank top, her hair piled up into a ponytail on top of her head.

Watching them interact caused him to smile, but the sudden happiness left him as Melissa took one of Avery's hands in hers. It was innocent and playful, but it startled him. Instinctively, he raised his hands to stop her but caught himself, the smile now gone. Melissa was unaware of his actions, though the sudden movement alerted her to his presence.

She turned to him, smiling, and walked towards him.

"Babe," she began seductively, "let's stay home today."

"C'mon, Lis," he replied uncomfortably as she moved closer and took his hands in hers.

"C'mon," she continued, "just you and me and Avery today. We never have any time together."

Aiden closed his eyes and breathed deeply. His hands felt good in hers. They were warm and soft, and her scent was sweet and light and uniquely her. He wanted to let himself go. He wanted to relax and feel free and safe. He wanted things the way they were before all of this. But Avery's small whimper brought him back to himself, back to his reality. He pulled away.

"We need to go," he told her, crossing the room to pick up his daughter, "this brunch was already planned."

"Fine," Melissa replied, frustrated.

"Why do you do that?" he asked.

"Do what?" she shot back. "What? Want to stay home? Want to spend time alone with my husband? Want to not always be over there?"

"Wow," he interrupted.

"I'm sick of it, I'm sick of being judged!" Melissa said angrily.

"Lilah worships you. She thinks that you are the saint of everything," he added sarcastically.

"I'm talking about your *mother*," she stated coldly.

Aiden began to speak but paused to consider his next words. He then spoke softly:

"Considering everything, I think she has been dealing with all of this very well."

Aiden was no fool. He was not blind to the tension between the two women. Cold contention. Forced politeness.

"Aiden, I have said I'm sorry a million times," she responded angrily. "I'm allowing this crazy routine, seeing a shrink, everything. I might as well be in jail, it would probably be better."

"You're allowing?" was all he replied.

"Just go," Melissa responded coldly. She turned away and walked out as Aiden picked up one of Avery's toys and handed it to her. He heard the bedroom door slam...

"I can't do it, Mom. Every time I look at her...it's not the same. She begs me to trust her, to let her have Avery back to get on with life. She says it is ridiculous and cruel to keep her away from her child. That she has a right to her baby and maybe she should just leave. Maybe she is right. I don't know. To me, she's just a monster who hurt my daughter. I don't trust her. I don't trust that I'm doing the right thing. I feel like such a fucking loser..."

"Why!!" Lilah shouted at them from the doorway. She had been listening from the kitchen. "Why would you keep this from me? I knew it, I just knew there was something else. But I believed you. I trusted you. Both of you. You lied to me."

They had not been careful. Neither knew what to say. They looked at each other, lost for words. Lex watched the color drain from Aiden's face.

"I don't want to lose Avery!" Lilah exclaimed. There was panic in the statement. "Will she take her? Why didn't you tell me the truth? How could you lie to me? My God, I'm not dead. She hurt my baby girl..."

"I'm sorry..." Lex began.

"Don't," Lilah stopped her and walked away.

Aiden rushed to go after her.

Lilah was right. What had their lives become?

4

Time was a slow-moving lonely companion. Time had no meaning and held all the power: time when Lilah was lucid, time when she slept. Never had Lex envisioned that Lilah's illness was hers as well. That all life would stop, and yet time would still move forward. Time took Lilah's good days with bad moments and changed them to bad days with good moments. Time dictated that mostly Lilah was medicated to a state of unconsciousness. Time now revolved around the coming and going of the hospice nurse, 10:30 to noon every day. Time brought breathing treatments and constant oxygen through a nasal cannula, and time most recently brought a hospice therapist once a week on Tuesday afternoons. This made very little sense to Lex, but nonetheless, he would come and quietly talk to Lilah and to her, and she let him talk, never really engaging and responding only enough to keep everything quiet and calm.

When Lilah was awake and when possible, Aiden would lay next to her with Avery between them for safety where her sweet Lilah, never at a loss for words, now struggled to speak, insisting on telling Avery how she would grow up to be an amazing woman, how she would always be watching over her. How her daddy loved her. The image burned itself painfully into Lex.

"Please, don't let anything happen to Avery, promise me," she begged Lex.

"Don't worry. I'm here..."

"I'm worried about Aiden," she interrupted weakly.

"He will be ok," Lex answered, stroking Lilah's face. "He's strong and passionate and full of life, like you."

"What about when I'm gone? Who will take care of you?"

"I will be ok, I promise," Lex lied, while thinking:

'I'm not ok. Nothing is ok. Everything is wrong, Lilah. I can't do this. I don't know what's happening. I don't know who I am anymore.'

Time was surreal; black and spiraling, an endless chasm of lost shadows, and they were all its trapped victims. Time played tricks on Lex, waking sometimes next to Lilah, and sometimes trapped in a childhood long past:

A basement staircase in her childhood home that was cold and hard where she sat at the top, listening through the closed hollow door to that slightly muffled sound between her and the kitchen. They waited in darkness, if not for the glow of the TV in the family room, it would have been blinding.

"What's happening?" her sister asked, her voice sweet and quiet.

She was standing at the bottom of the stairs, wide-eyed through the crooked bangs of her pixie cut hair. Her clothes were mismatched from quickly pulling on red polyester pants under her yellow flower nightgown, ready to escape if they needed to.

Lexi's hair was similar; same crooked bangs but long and unbrushed, and just as mismatched, but not pajamas, which were too risky and unprepared.

38

"I can't hear nothing...the dryer is too loud," her sister said quietly.

It was true, the dryer banged in detached rhythm; tennis shoes mixed in with the laundry.

"Go watch TV," the nine-year-old version of Lexi ordered.

"No, I wanna hear, too."

Lexi weighed this in her head...listen to her sister pout and whine or let her up to hear the frightening, violent yelling match. She motioned for her to come up.

"What are they doing?" she asked.

"Fighting, duh."

A loud bang hit the door and startled them, almost causing them to fall backwards in fear.

"What was that?" her sister asked quickly.

"Coffee cup. I think," Lexi replied.

"Ima watch TV," her sister said, crawling down the stairs with her thumb in her mouth, her eyes wide with fear. She picked up her blanket and ran the silky edge through her fingers.

"Go ahead," Lexi told her, "don't worry, it will be ok."

She continued to listen, biting her fingernails, what was left of them, and wondering if it was indeed going to be ok. They were trapped in the basement. There was no other way out. The chair she had propped up to the family room window was gone, and she knew she couldn't reach it to escape. She could lift her sister up, though, enough for her to open the window. If she could push out the screen, then she could crawl out. She just wouldn't be able to lift herself up to get out, too. The fighting continued...

Lex stared up at the ceiling as Lilah slept. So many nights of sleep interrupted by the nightmares that tormented her, first in her subconscious, then in those first waking moments as she was jolted from sleep, sweaty and panicked, frightened like a child and Lilah's declining health always looming dark.

'Don't do it, Lex.'

She caught her breath. Lilah did not stir. She looked so peaceful, so content...which Lex surmised was more likely the result of the amount of medication she was on than actual contentment. She watched her sleep as she calmed herself, reaching over to gently brush her fingers through the sleeping woman's hair.

'Don't do it Lex.'

That very old and familiar numbness constantly plagued her, first in her stomach then in her chest. She eased quietly out of bed, motioning for the dog to follow her to the living room. As she curled up on the sofa, the dog yawned and stared up at her patiently, wagging his tail, waiting to be invited up. Lex patted the cushion next to her, and he jumped up, laid down and drifted off to sleep. Wishing that sleep came to her that easily, she picked up the keyboard from the ottoman and opened an interface in the game she created, reaching out for someone, anyone, who could get her what she needed, something to stop the nightmares, to give her back her life.

She waited...

The remaining cooler first weeks of Spring ended, warming into days of Spring rain. Lilah slept more often than she was awake, and when she was awake, she was often disoriented. The reality that any day could be their last consumed Lex. It didn't feel sad...it was just a heavy sterile reality.

It had become too difficult, and Lilah's needs were too unpredictable for Avery to be at the house now, much to Melissa's delight. Both she and her therapist thought it was time for things to return to a more normal routine for both Avery and Melissa. Without missing a beat, and to Aiden's (and Melissa's) surprise, Lex agreed:

"We have to trust the process, Aiden," she told him, "We can't keep living in this constant state of uncertainty. If this therapist truly believes she is in a good place, then now really is a good time."

She sensed his uncertainty.

"You've spoken with him, and you've had sessions together. You have to decide for yourself if this makes sense," she added. She knew that her opinion, her support, held a lot of weight and would make it easier for him.

Lex stood at the window watching the rain stream down the glass; each small drop sounding like the tick of tapping fingernails. Behind her, Lilah had just drifted off to sleep. It would be hours before she woke again.

'Don't,' she thought.

"No one will notice," she muttered softly to herself.

From between the mattresses, she retrieved a small pouch and put it in her purse. Silently, quickly, she grabbed her keys and left the house.

The drive would be short, and Lex paid little attention to the road or traffic. Music haunted quietly from the radio:

"...Oh, Father tell me, do we get what we deserve..." -Kaleo

Lex drove mechanically. She watched cars, street signs; she stopped for traffic on queue. But this was all from habit: Lex wasn't there.

'What if she had pulled the trigger and shot you?' her mother's voice haunted.

'She wouldn't have,' he had laughed.

'You don't know that. Everyone's life would be ruined.'

'There is no way she would shoot me. She's too scared.'

He had been right. Lexi was too scared. He had seen it in her eyes when she pointed the gun from the stairs as he walked by, the gun shaking in her small hands. It had been a particularly nasty fight, and Lexi didn't remember getting the gun. He had stopped only briefly and stared at her. The gaze told the same truth...he owned them. He turned with a small laugh and walked out. He could do whatever he wanted. Everything that followed was her fault for not protecting them...

A cold drop of rain hit Lex on the cheek, and as it rolled down her jawline, she realized her hair was wet.

'How long have I been standing here?' she thought, shivering.

Lex contemplated her next actions as she looked down at the doorknob. Her hands shook as she reached forward: From the chill of the rain? She didn't know. For just a moment, she felt panic rise through her. She caught her breath and knocked.

"Hey!" came the exclamation from her daughter-in-law. "Come on in," Melissa said, nervously picking up a few clothes off the sofa.

"I came to talk," Lex said.

"Ok," Melissa said with uncertainty.

Lex smiled at her uneasiness, and any remaining panic was replaced with a quiet calm.

"You look worried. Everything is fine, Melissa," she said quietly.

Melissa seemed to sigh in relief.

"Do you want something to drink?" she offered.

"Water, sure," she answered, following her to the kitchen.

As the young woman reached for a couple glasses, Lex said, "Actually, let's have something stronger."

"What's wrong?" the young woman asked cautiously.

"Nothing."

Lex could sense Melissa's nervousness: She could hear it in her breathing, saw it in her movements. She got to the point.

"I think it's time for us to be honest with each other," she said as Melissa chose glassware from the cupboard.

"Then you're right, we should have a drink," Melissa responded, pouring bourbon into each glass.

From the other room, Avery began to cry.

Lex smiled at her, "Go on, I'll get these."

Melissa left to attend to Avery, and when she returned several minutes later, Lex had made her way to the sofa.

"All good?" Lex asked. "C'mon, sit. Let's have a chat."

"I'm doing better, you know," Melissa stated, sitting on the opposite end of the sofa. "Dr. Glenn says that I need to work on my anger issues, from when I was a kid, you know, keep it in check, but that I'm really handling it."

"Hmm." Lex raised her glass and swallowed the liquid.

Hesitantly, Melissa did the same.

"Ugh...I've never quite liked the taste of Bourbon," Lex commented. "I don't understand why you and Aiden like it."

Lex searched her soul, her experiences for some reason to stop this. What excuse could there be? Just a year ago, they would have been laughing and engaged. A lifetime had passed since then.

'Don't do it, Lex.'

"From when we met," Melissa explained, "at the end of a party. It was almost morning, and Aiden asked if I wanted a drink, and there was just an almost empty bottle of bourbon. I don't know if either of us really like it. It just is what it is..."

Melissa felt warm and light and more buzzed than she normally would.

"So, why are you here?" she asked abruptly.

"You're not taking my grandchild," Lex stated with quiet calm.

"I don't know..." Melissa started to say, though Lex cut her off quickly:

"Stop. You know what I do, what I did for a living right?"

Melissa didn't respond.

Lex sighed before responding. The alcohol burned in her stomach.

"May seven, United Airlines, two seats. Traveling with infant. One way to Maryland."

"She's my baby," Melissa responded harshly but quietly. "You...you guys think you can take her from me, treat me like, what? A distant relative? Think you can keep her from me."

"Yes," Lex replied calmly as she rubbed the back of her neck and watched Melissa, "really I do."

Melissa's heart was beating faster, and she was sweating now. Her eyes widened.

'No. This can't happen, Lex. You have to stop this.'

"...And way down we go...." -Kaleo

Lex looked down at her watch, ignoring the voice in her head, wondering how long this would take.

"I saw you, you know. That day at the hospital." Lex was calm, relaxed as she watched the woman in front of her struggle to calm herself, to breathe.

Aiden would be home soon. She thought she would feel something, maybe scared, maybe panicked. Instead, she just felt calm. Too calm. Perhaps it was the alcohol, and Lex made a mental note to remember that.

'I missed it,' Lex thought as Melissa struggled, *'all that time with my son, with us, and I totally missed it, never even tried to find out who she really was, never doubted her story about her parents, her siblings.'*

Lex had trusted her to be the person she said she was, and she lied.

Melissa struggled to speak, "I don't..."

"No, Melissa, just stop," Lex commanded. "I've seen it before, you know...that damaged, dangerous look. It can't be fixed...even the sweetest dogs, the most loyal...sometimes they attack. It's primal, instinctive."

Melissa tried to speak. Her heart hurt, it felt like it was exploding.

Lex approached her and cupped her face in her hands gently, and Melissa grabbed onto her wrists, digging her fingernails into the cotton of Lex's shirt sleeves. Lex looked her in the eyes, smiled and quietly continued:

"Shh. It's ok. The difference is, you're not supposed to be an animal, and I think, maybe, you would have made the right choice if you could, but you bent that baby's fingers back, one at a time, each one snapped in a different place. Not an accident, not a quick, angry outburst. And now, taking Avery from us, from my son..."

Lex stopped talking as she felt Melissa's grip loosen and watched her slip into unconsciousness.

Lex pulled gloves from her pocket and took a syringe of liquid from her purse. Carefully, she tied the woman's arm, found a vein, and after a few unsuccessful attempts, plunged the needle through. She took Melissa's opposite hand and placed her thumb make-shift on the plunger and pushed the liquid into her arm. As she let go of her hand, the needle fell to the floor.

She put the pouch containing the remaining vile of heroin on the table next to the empty glass, picked hers up, washed it and put it back in the cabinet.

She checked for a pulse. There was none. Lex leaned over Melissa's lifeless body and pushed the hair back out of her face. She looked peaceful now that she was asleep forever; this pathetic, pretty lost girl who had charmed her son, charmed them all really. For a moment, she felt compassion for this creature, and only for a moment as a chill rose from her neck and into her brain.

'I'm not like you. I don't hurt innocent, helpless creatures,' she thought.

Lex checked on Avery, who slept soundly and unaffected with her mother dead in the next room. She again checked her watch, hopeful that Aiden would leave work on time, gambling that he would and that the child would only be alone for a short time and then never again.

"We were patient, weren't we, Sweet Girl?" she quietly told the sleeping infant.

In the car, she reached for her phone instinctively but stopped herself, choosing not to turn it back on in case there was ever a question about her whereabouts. It was as she checked her mirror to back out that she noticed her eyes: They were red and wet with tears that she had no time for.

By the time Lex rushed through her front door, the tears were gone. She laid down on the bed next to Lilah and ran her fingers over her arm, watching her sleep, waiting.

How this would affect her son, affect them all, she didn't know. She hadn't thought about the consequence until this quiet moment, but it wouldn't have mattered even if she knew: Melissa was dead from that moment at the hospital all those months prior. Lex had compared Melissa to an animal, but really, this was not at all fair. After all, it was Lex who had attacked. She couldn't be fixed. The phone rang.

"Aiden, sweetheart what's wrong..."

He blamed himself for not paying attention. He was too angry, and in his indifference, stopped looking. How could she do this? Especially now? It was so selfish. Where would she even get the drugs? She had said that she came from a family of addicts, she swore she would never touch the stuff.

"My God...this is unbelievable," she told him mechanically. "Is Avery....oh my god Avery, is she ok?"

"She's fine," Aiden reassured.

"I thought she was making progress.," Lex continued, "she seemed so much better. I'm coming over..."

"No, there is nothing you can do," Aiden interrupted, his voice cracking and quiet. "Stay with Mom. I'll come there when the police finish. They have questions..."

5

In the nights that followed, the long agonizing nights after the call, after the tragedy and tears, Lex would lay awake, fearing sleep. Not because of Melissa: She felt nothing for doing what had to be done. Lex was terrified that every breath would be Lilah's last. That she would be sleeping when Lilah finally died. Selfishly, she wanted every moment.

"Mom, is it ok if we don't say anything about Melissa?" Aiden had asked. "I don't know how to tell her."

Lex agreed; what would be the point? She was in and out so much now.

'That was the plan,' she thought.

Sitting in the darkness, the silence was loud. Lex could hear her own heartbeat. Across the house, Aiden and Avery slept; Aiden unable to go back to the place where his wife had died.

"Lilah," Lex whispered, crying softly. "I'm so sorry it's you. You are so much better at all of this. You deserve our family, our life. I don't know who to be without us. How can you just go? It's not right. It's not fair. You promised me forever, remember?"

Their relationship had been unexpected, at least, it was to Lex:

She was 18 and working on a final essay in the library when Lilah first approached her:

"Can I sit here?"

Lex looked up, and there she was, hair pulled back behind her ears with a rolled pink bandana tied in a small bow on top of her head, lips glossy and tinted red, long button-down white shirt with a thick pink belt sitting just at the waist and a tight pink skirt. At the time, Lex hadn't realized how long she had studied the girl before nodding yes.

"Cool, thanks," Lilah said, dropping her books on the table as she sat across from her. "God, finals are such a killer, right?"

"Yes, I suppose," Lex answered.

She extended her hand across the table, "I'm Lilah."

Hesitantly, Lex took her hand, simply responding, "Lex."

"What are you studying?" she asked.

"Cobal, Fortran, C+," Lex replied.

"C+, like the grade?"

"C+, like the computer language," Lex stated.

"Ohhh, that C+," Lilah said with a little laugh.

"You ready to go?" a familiar male voice asked Lex, putting his hands on her shoulders.

Lex looked up.

"Yes, absolutely," she replied, standing.

"This is my boyfriend, Cody," she told Lilah.

"Hey," Cody said with a nod.

"Oh. Hi," Lilah said absently.

"Let's go, we're going to miss the bus," he insisted.

"Ok, got it," Lex told him sarcastically, turning back to Lilah, "See you around."

"You will," the young woman replied.

"What was that about?" Cody asked her as they hurried to the bus.

"What was what about?"

"You don't know who that is?"

Lex had seen her before but shook her head indicating that she did not know her.

"That is Lilah Vance."

The statement meant nothing to Lex.

Cody continued, "She's probably the most popular girl in your college."

"How would you know?" she asked him.

"You don't remember her speech on immigration in the quad? It was on every channel," Cody remarked.

"No, but who cares?" she asked.

"What did she want?" he demanded.

"Nothing. She just asked if she could sit at the table," Lex answered, annoyed at the interrogation.

"Well, she looked more engaged than that," he commented.

"Cody, what does that even mean? I'm not selling secrets for fuck's sake."

"Fine," he said, annoyed.

She and Coty fought a lot: over money, over code, over how much time Lex should spend writing code. They had a fight that evening. Looking back, Lex realized the fight wasn't about any of that. Cody saw something that she hadn't. Lilah was competition, and he wasn't having it.

Regardless, Lilah was there in the library the next day and the next, and Lex, who preferred to be alone most of the time, found herself looking forward to spending time with her. First it was just the library, then lunch a few times a week, then an occasional movie.

Lilah told her how her mother had died when she was young, and though she and her dad were very close, she confided that she always felt a little sad growing up without a mom. Lex loved her passionate anger over social injustices and how she was studying to be a pharmaceutical scientist, how she wanted to help develop easily accessible medications for third world countries.

When Lex and Cody fought, which was often, Lilah listened to her complain without judgement. Ironically, the more time Lex spent with Lilah instead of on the computer, the more she and Cody fought.

Theirs had been a relationship of need and convenience, a means to an end. Before Cody, Lex had been alone. He made her feel less alone. When it was good, it was great, when it was bad…it wasn't great. He always came back, always apologized. It wasn't violent, but it wasn't stable. Lex honestly believed that she couldn't live without him. At least she existed to him. It was true that he was taking advantage of her. She didn't care. It was better than being alone.

Until Lilah. Until there was a world outside of sitting in front of a computer. It was more than that: there was life *beyond* the computer. Lex had spent the majority of her life observing, believing that there was no place for her in real life and yet here she was going to events, laughing more, less alone even by herself. Now she felt the most alone whenever she was with Cody. She tried to hide it, afraid to lose him. She didn't love him, didn't need him. He was her only connection to the real world. Maybe that was by design: she had an excuse not to interact with people.

More and more, it reminded her of every relationship she had ever observed as a child. And it had worked for her. And now it didn't. So, what started as tolerance for Cody's attitude whenever Lilah came over to pick her up morphed into Cody often trying to keep her from leaving. This had escalated, and it wasn't really a surprise to Lex one evening when she was supposed to be meeting Lilah at the library, and Cody physically blocked the door, shouting at her:

"I've had enough of this, Lex!" he shouted, "I don't want you to see her anymore."

Lex laughed at him and responded, "Wow. Get out of the way, I'm already running late."

"No. I'm serious, stay here or I'm leaving for good," he demanded.

"Fine," she yelled at him, heading to the window.

"Oh, hell no!" he responded, grabbing her arm tightly.

Instinctively, she turned around and punched him in the nose, causing him to let go, and they both fell; him against the wall and her over a coffee table and with it all of the items on the table.

"Fucking fuck, Lex, you broke my nose!" he said as blood dripped down his face.

Cody picked up a glass and threw it at her. She caught it and threw it back as she got up off the floor. He moved quickly, and it shattered as it hit the wall next to him.

"That's it! I'm leaving!" he shouted.

"I don't care," she responded, realizing as she said it that she really didn't. He broke the rules by grabbing her.

"I mean it, Lex, I'm not coming back ever," he threatened.

"I already said I don't care."

"What is it with her, huh? Are you fucking her?"

"No," Lex replied, controlling the anger, "But maybe I will. So fucking go."

"Maybe I'll have a little talk with her," he said then, seeming desperate to take back control of the conversation.

"Get out, Cody, and stay away from her. And me," she ordered.

"You need me," Cody told her.

"Not like this, not anymore. Fucking how much money are you making from my work? Huh? My work, what I can do. Me," she emphasized quietly, adding, "You won't go near Lilah because I know the same people you do, and I have something they want and you don't. So back the fuck off."

Cody seemed scared. Or maybe shocked. She'd called his bluff and sealed it with a "I have all the power" response. As they stood staring at each other, they both knew it.

"I'm sorry," he told her, "I didn't mean to grab you..."

"But you did, Cody. You promised you would never do that, and you did. You have to go," she responded.

Cody turned around and walked out without another word, and as Lex bolted the door, she let out a long breath then collapsed to the floor, crying.

"...I was the game he would play. He brought the clouds to my day." -The Jets

She didn't have a sense of how long she sat there...long enough to stop crying, long enough to think about never seeing him again and how sad it made her feel.

Someone knocked lightly at the door.

"Lex?" It was Lilah. With everything that just happened, she had forgotten the whole reason the fight even started.

"Lex! Lex, are you ok? Let me in!" her voice sounded panicked.

Lex slid the door open slightly.

"Oh my god, Lex, I thought something happened to you, then I saw blood in the hallway..."

Lilah stopped talking abruptly as she took in Lex's tear-soaked face, and as Lex opened the door, she caught a glimpse of her arm, bruised with what looked like fingerprints and what appeared to be blood on her hand. She saw the broken items and more blood.

"WHAT THE FUCK?" she yelled out, which caused Lex to start crying again.

Lilah pulled her into a hug, continuing to scan the room, then pushed her back and looked her over saying, "Where are you hurt?"

"I'm not," Lex replied

"Lex, there is blood everywhere..."

"It's Cody's. I punched him in the nose," she said in a matter-of-fact tone.

"Where is he?" Lilah asked, scanning the room.

"He's gone," Lex said wistfully. "Forever, I think."

Lilah grabbed her hand and tried to pull her towards the door. "You think? C'mon, let's get out of here."

"Why?" Lex asked, stopping her.

"You don't have to stay here with him," she answered.

"This is my place," Lex tried to explain.

"You'll find another one," Lilah interrupted.

Lex motioned her to the sofa, and Lilah complied hesitantly.

"Lilah, I mean this is my apartment, not his. I pay for it, not him."

Lilah struggled with her reply:

"I thought...I mean..."

"...that I'm some helpless little girl?" Lex finished her sentence.

"No...yes," Lilah stated, "not helpless. Ugh, I don't know what I thought. If this is your place, I don't know, I don't get it, are you afraid of him? We should go to the police..."

Lex held up her hands, motioning her to stop talking.

"Look. One, I can take care of myself..."

"Questionable," Lilah commented.

"...I can take care of myself. Trust me, he won't be back. I have people invested in me being ok."

Lex remembered Lilah being genuinely confused.

"Ok, I really need to know what that is about, but right now, I just want to know that you are ok for real. If you're hurt. I mean, you were crying."

"I'll miss him," Lex stated with a sigh. "We have...history."

The look on Lilah's face told Lex that she didn't, couldn't, understand, and Lex was grateful for that, for someone not like him, or for that matter, like her.

"Then like a ray of light. You came my way one night."

"Never mind. I'm not hurt," she told her.

Cody would never come back, and that was her doing. Sometimes Lex longed to talk to him, to be for a moment with someone who understood her.

It took Lex a year: a year of living alone, a year of their friendship to ask Lilah out on a real date, and it ended up being Lilah who instigated their first kiss, Lilah who was brave and unafraid of a relationship.

"I promise I will never leave you," she told Lex.

Lex smiled at the memory of her own awkward insecurity, that song stuck in her head as she held Lilah closer.

When Lilah finally took her last breath, Lex felt sorrow slip into numbness. Lilah hadn't been alive for days. There was no spoken goodbye, no last words. What was said had already been said. Lex watched Aiden gently stroke his mother's hair and kiss her cheek for the last time, and she felt her heart pounding in her ears. Around her, people spoke, and she watched the words coming out of their mouths, but the sound escaped her. She went through the motions, answered questions, allowed herself to be hugged, heard her own voice across a chasm.

The funeral service was not real to her because there was no reality, it was mechanical, sterile. There was no sadness. There was only selfish rage. And after, when she was all alone and the dark night was filled with overwhelming deafening silence, Lex sat in the corner of their bedroom, arms around her knees, gripping a plastic flash drive cover with a small sticky note attached, the cold of the nothingness surrounding her:

'Lex- Remember to be hopeful. I love you forever and beyond. –Lilah'

In the darkness, she listened as Lilah's voice resonated from the computer, slicing like a knife through the silence:

"Lexi, everything I should say, everything I should have said but never did swirls in my mind these days. I remember everything..."

"For who I am without you...forgive me, my love," Lex said out loud, broken and sobbing as Lilah's voice continued.

"...and way down we go." -Kaleo

After...

6

'...I keep your photograph, I know it serves me well. I want to hold you high and steal your pain.' -Seether

With Lilah gone, time drifted. It was one month, then three, summer to winter, then the next summer and the next. For a while, as each new day started, just before reality, there was that brief second that held their broken perfection. Now, those moments were rare. She reminded herself often that Lilah was no longer in pain, and that kept the constant quiet rage of her death from turning to bitterness. Lilah's love had been pure, unbreaking and irreplaceable. The pictures and the objects of their lives stood unchanged throughout their home as a reminder of this. There were new pictures, new 'things,' but everything from before remained.

"Gramma, the game won't work!"

Lex smiled as she diced vegetables. The tiny voice shouting from the living room once again saved her from her thoughts. Just outside the kitchen window, the dog chased a blue jay back and forth in the late morning summer sun. The blue jay, who appeared to be enjoying the dog's struggle, flew just out of reach. They were both relentless: the bird dive-bombing and the dog jumping and barking.

Lex functioned now for Aiden, for Avery. And only for them. In the moments alone, she was broken and empty, but they kept her sane. And the dog kept her sane. Or maybe not quite sane as she talked to him as if he understood her. How lucky was his life, revolving around a ball? And Avery loved him.

Aiden had struggled adjusting to life as a single father at first, and it was his struggle that allowed Lex to put hers aside and guide him through this sorrowful maze. Mostly for him, it was the guilt of wishing for some way out when Melissa was alive that did not involve losing Avery. And when she was dead... why didn't he see it coming? Maybe he didn't want to. He'd admitted to Lex that he lived with the fear that Avery would disappear forever.

How close to right he had been.

His grief for Lilah, however, had overshadowed his grief for his wife. Towards Melissa, he expressed a silent disgust. Lex knew the timing of it all was unfair, but whatever guilt she had was replaced with justification. She had promised Lilah that nothing would happen to Avery. That Aiden would be ok.

Together, they had picked up the pieces of their fragmented life. He was so much Lilah's child, and Lex watched his grief begin to fade, his heart heal and his smile return just as she held onto her own grief as if it was all that kept her breathing.

At first, he stayed with her, opting not to sleep in the home he and Melissa shared and that she had just died in. Then he stayed because with Lilah so close to death, it made sense for him to be there with her. After, it made sense for him to stay. It was comforting to fill the silence that only death can bring. Lex had needed this more than she allowed herself to admit.

As one month turned to three and then five, in spite of Lex wanting to keep them close, keep them safe, she knew that Aiden wouldn't be able to truly move forward unless he took that next step. He had reluctantly agreed, and though he expressed concern leaving Lex alone, she knew that part of him was afraid of being alone with Avery.

Once he found a new place, though, and decorated a room for Avery and moved his things, he realized that his mother had been right. It felt good to have his own space again. It felt good to bring Avery home after work, to a home he was making for her.

They found the balance in their lives. Sometimes they ate together, sometimes not. Sometimes he'd spend whole days, weekends, just he and Avery. Sometimes he'd spend a few days alone or with friends. The remaining pain and emptiness faded, and he was grateful to have his mom always thinking one step ahead. He rediscovered himself and rediscovered love.

When Aiden told Lex this one afternoon, confirming what she could already see in his eyes, she felt part of the tightness in her chest began to ease; in spite of wanting them to need her more, she let go. Except for watching Avery.

"Mom, there's a daycare at the hospital, I was thinking..."

"No," she responded quickly.

"You should have your life back."

"No, no daycare."

On that topic, Lex was adamant.

For a time, Lexi and her sister attended a home-based multi-care babysitter before school and right after. The woman, that Nazi of a woman, kept them in her "furnished" basement while she stayed upstairs with the infants. They lived their time in a semi-finished holding cell of forgotten children. They weren't allowed on the stairs nor could they call out to her. That would mean sitting in a corner chair, forgotten for what could be hours or even a day.

On the cruel days of no school and all of that summer, lunch was provided. Soup. Always the same, some type of vegetable soup and then a metal cup of powdered milk. It was a painful experience for Lexi, who was cursed as a child to be a picky eater. And that soup was the worst on the planet in her mind. Sometimes someone would be lucky enough to have brought their own lunch, oh how the rest would sit and watch in envy of that kid eating a good PB&J or meat sandwich with potato chips. And what was that, a Ding Dong? The envy...

Lunchtime, and all children were lined up at a picnic table bench and a bowl of Steaming Hell placed in front of them. They were not allowed to leave the table until every last drop was licked clean. Lexi was usually the last one sitting at the table, typically for an extra half hour to an hour, the soup cold and slimy before she would gag down the last bit of that re-warmed vomit. She was quite often yelled at and often made fun of by other kids, led by the Nazi woman's teenage daughter, Nazi Jr., who was in charge of physically watching them and knowing Lexi's distaste for her mother's soup, Jr. was sure to see that she got a nice full bowl, served with that same laugh. After soup, and because she was last left at the table, Lexi often had to retrieve the metal cup of powdered milk from the open pantry area. She considered herself lucky because the metal kept the milk cold enough to tolerate.

In the summer, there weren't enough spaces on the floor to sleep, so older kids were made to sit with their heads down at the lunch table, and they were not allowed up until they had slept. Nazi Jr. got to determine if sleep occurred and if it was for a long enough duration. Lexi never took a single nap. It was far too dangerous to be unconscious and vulnerable. She did just as she did at home: pretended to sleep.

She learned not to respond if Jr. was whispering about her to another child. She practiced responding slowly when Jr. would walk to the door, open it and announce, "Your mom is here." Hardest of all, Lexi learned not to flinch like a conscious person if Jr. came up behind her and pinched the underside of her arm. It took time to get it right, and often her mother would come to pick them up with Lexi still sitting at the table. Eventually, no one was as good as she was at faking sleep. No one ever asked why she was sitting at a picnic table with her head down.

If she could have complied, she would have been less of a target. Something in her couldn't. Every weekday morning of that summer and Christmas break and spring break, she would wake and a familiar tightness would form in her stomach. Lexi would beg her mom to pack a lunch. She remembered those words:

"Part of what I am paying for is lunch."

And that was that.

Such an odd thing to stress about. Her stomach would get tighter throughout the morning as she obsessed about the horror show of the day so that by lunch, she was completely stressed out and nauseous. No, she wasn't grateful to at least have food. Yes, she cared about starving children and would have been quite happy to skip that meal in support of there being more food to share with them.

The whole memory, like so many others, had been lost to her for years. Another faded image left behind and replaced by her life with Lilah. But now? The world had already cracked in so many places. The smell of vegetable soup made her nauseous. The only time she would drink milk was standing in the kitchen. Weird idiosyncrasies that required no explanation with Lilah, so they were allowed to become that: just small personality quirks and not some physical tortured connection to childhood.

So much had returned, opening fresh wounds.

At Nazi Daycare, Jr. and Lexi had a come here - go away relationship. It really depended on her status that day with Jr.'s younger sister, who was around her age and once in a while grew bored upstairs in the Forbidden Zone, so she would come down. She ruled their world when she came to play, because with one statement or misstep, she could disappear and take her good toys with her, and they would be left with broken baby toys and a TV that could only be watched if Jr. felt like it.

The sisters were often at war with each other and took every opportunity to get everyone involved, creating daily factions, baiting kids against each other. It was during those times that Jr.'s attention was the worst, and Lexi felt helpless. She had to do what she was told. Those were the times when Jr.'s eyes grew darker and a smile would curl on her face as she called Lexi over to sit on her lap. And Lexi always did, even though she knew it wasn't right, that it never ended well. Lexi just disappeared into someone else, watching, saying, *"No, don't go over there,"* but not listening.

In her soul, she could see young Lexi straddle Jr., facing her, hearing her make fun of everything about her: her hair, her eyes, nose, teeth, what she was wearing, sarcastically and methodically tearing her down into nothing:

"You always wear the same clothes; you're too poor and ugly so no one buys you any new ones."

And worse:

"You should start wearing a bra," and Jr. would grab and twist her breasts, which happened so often that Lexi would still be sore from the day before when it would happen again. It was only for that reason, when the robot self couldn't bear it any longer, that one day Lexi cut her off, grabbing Jr.'s breasts and twisting, holding on with a death grip. Jr. had to stand up and drop Lexi off her lap to get her to let go. She had fallen to the floor, hitting her head on the tile, but it was worth it: It never happened again...

"But mom," Aiden told her in that calm, Lilah manner, "you need to move on, have your life back, go back to work, get out of the house and live."

"I am living," she'd told him then. "I don't want to go back to work, and I don't need to. Being with Avery is me moving on. I promise. This makes me happy."

This wasn't completely a lie. Her only real happiness, a laugh or a smile, was because of Avery: her first steps, words...holding her close and telling her stories about Grandma Lilah, watching Aiden as a father. This was the promise to Lilah and as much of it as she could keep.

This was also the only time she felt the remnants of before when everything was good. When she was alone, Lex had become someone else.

"Gramma!"

"Bring me the controller," Lex called back from the kitchen.

The frustrated, sandy blonde four-year-old handed over the controller.

"The bear won't move," she pouted, crossing her little arms across her chest.

Lex put the controller on the counter.

"Here," she said, pulling over a chair, "Come up here and help me make lunch."

"I wanna play," Avery whined.

"Hey, you can play later. The bear needs a break. Let's wash your hands, and you can make this salad."

The 'game,' perfected over time, was in the middle of an upgrade.

Lex watched her granddaughter tear tiny pieces of lettuce from a wedge, placing each piece in the larger bowl carefully, slowly.

"I like your earrings," Lex told her, "they make you look so grown up."

Avery delighted in the compliment.

"Allison got me them at the mall yesterday," she said.

"You like her a lot, don't you?" she asked the child, who responded:

"Ya, Gramma. Daddy said she is going to live with us."

Avery paused.

"Gramma?"

"Hmm?"

"Is Allison my mommy now?" Avery asked her.

Lex sighed, not sure how to reply. Allison had come into Aiden's life just as it seemed he needed it most. In the months following Lilah's passing, as he finished his surgical residency and she was completing hers. In Psychiatry. She liked the young woman, and whereas Lex mistrusted the profession, she often found herself amused by the young woman's wicked sense of humor. That and the white rabbit tattoo on one arm and playing cards on the other. Lex had taken to calling her Alice out loud. She found that she couldn't help herself and meant no offense by it, but how could she be expected not to?

"Her name is Allison, she has a white rabbit on her arm, and you seriously expect me not to think '*Alice in Wonderland*'?" she had told Aiden when he had confronted her, frustrated that Lex never addressed Allison as he thought she should.

"I don't mind if you call me Alice," Allison told her candidly one day. "I'm sure everyone thinks it, they just don't say it out loud."

They had married recently, and though Avery knew this, she didn't quite understand what that really meant to her. That Aiden moved on and could laugh was what counted most to Lex. It was selfish, she knew, but the relief that Aiden found someone new felt like a burden lifted, like she did right by him, all of them. At least that's what she had convinced herself.

Still, Lex kept a respectful distance, but this time, she did a background check. Allison didn't have family, her parents having perished in a fire, all completely verifiable, which Lex made sure to do this time. This seemed to make her profession understandable. She had a certain mystery to her, a darkness, but nothing evil. She was genuinely sweet. Aiden was happy, Avery was happy. She seemed controllable. That was that.

"Do you want her to be?" she asked Avery.

"Is she gonna die?" Avery asked innocently.

"Why do you say that?"

Avery grew still and silent.

"Avery?"

Lex saw her little pink lips quiver, and she started to sob.

Lex scooped her up.

"Sweet Girl, what happened?" she soothed quietly.

"I don't want her to die like my borned mom."

'Fuck.'

"Avery, look at me. Look at Grandma," Lex coaxed. "Hey. Allison is not going to die. I promise."

Lex had no right to say it. Who was she to state the future for anyone and lie to the child?

"Your mom was sick, remember, I told you that?"

Avery nodded, "Like Grandma Lilah."

"Not like Grandma Lilah. Grandma Lilah was a different sick," Lex replied carefully. Even Avery's innocent reference to Melissa and Lilah being the same angered her. She regrouped quickly.

"Allison is not sick," she pointed out. "I think she loves you and Daddy. Did she say something?"

Avery nodded. "I asked her, and she said she would be my mommy but only if I wanted her to."

This was not a conversation Lex wanted to have. It felt uncomfortable. One day Avery might know the truth, that Lex had taken her mother from her. She avoided the consequence of that day and made a mental note to speak with Aiden and Allison. All of this was theirs to explain, not hers. The advantage of being a grandparent. And soon enough, both of their lives would begin to change, but that was for another day.

"I love you, you know that, right?" Lex asked.

Avery nodded.

"Okay, then. You don't have to worry about anything. Allison isn't going to die, because I say so. If you want her to be your mommy, then she can be your mommy."

Avery seemed satisfied with the response and went back to tearing up little pieces of lettuce, singing out loud to herself. Relieved, Lex took the last two pills from a bottle in a high cupboard and swallowed them without water.

Late that evening, Lex sat on the sofa in the dark with a keyboard in her lap. For a while, she watched the dog sleep, his chest rising and falling softly. She opened a link and scrolled through the news. Simultaneously, she opened a game session, and a 'dark net' window popped up. She searched for new postings. There was always something to occupy her...find account information on a business partner, hack accounts, create a backdoor into a business for a virus. She sighed at the lack of challenge.

She didn't need the money. Lex could manipulate investments, funnel money to private untraceable accounts; she'd done all of that the first year after Lilah died. Their home was paid off long before Lilah got sick. Between Lilah's life insurance and pension, there was no financial need to work. The truth was that she could not bear to go back to work after Lilah died. She was obsessed with controlling her world.

She hadn't come to that conclusion on her own. A therapist told her she was compensating for grief by trying to control her surroundings (if only he really knew what she was doing). Lex owned it. So what? It was satisfying to anonymously leave a tip that led to a criminal, a child pornographer, a contract killer. Or when someone was getting financially screwed over? It was divine intervention. Maybe not divine, but awesome at least. Lilah would have never approved, but just maybe she would understand if it was for the greater good. At least, that was how Lex justified it to make it acceptable.

When she did accept a 'paying job,' it was almost always one asshole wanting to fuck over another asshole, usually over a financial dispute. Financial men, or women; she didn't mind taking money from rich people trying to stay rich. She convinced herself that taking money was investing in Avery's future.

Lilah had been wrong when she said this wasn't her. This had always been her. It was Lilah that made her want to be different, let her pretend to be someone else. A lifetime ago. Lilah had filled the endless dark spiraling void until she died. No, that was too simple and disrespected their life. Lilah was so much more. Now, Lex was on the path that perhaps she was always meant to be on: filling the hours with the addiction of controlling and manipulating others because she could, waiting for the next challenge, the high never quite good enough, but just enough to keep from going crazy. Living for the promise to Lilah. If not for Aiden and her granddaughter, she would not be alive. Another fact she owned.

Lex accepted that she was going to Hell, if there was one, but she didn't care. Her promise to Lilah, though, to make sure they were ok, make sure they were safe, she had to keep it.

She clicked a posting and began to read when another window beeped and popped open.

"Hello," appeared in white.

"Hi," she typed back.

"I got your message. What can I do for you?" the doctor, maybe a doctor, with a screen name LilyQ asked.

Lex switched to voice over, saying "I'm out of medicine."

"Already?" the computerized voice asked.

"Yes."

In the first months after Lilah died, Lex began having severe panic attacks. At first, she thought it was something else. They had never been this bad in the past, and it was only after Aiden found her sitting on the floor against the kitchen wall, sweat soaked and gasping for air, only after she had lied to him, saying it had never happened before, only after he "convinced her" to be admitted for tests that this was confirmed. To her disappointment, she discovered that she was indeed not dying.

Before she was discharged, she found herself sitting silently across from a psychiatrist, who sat just as silent.

"What am I supposed to say?" she asked him finally.

"I think you are having panic attacks in response to the loss of your wife. Many people experience this in place of grief," the doctor said matter-of-factly.

When Lex didn't respond, he continued:

"I think you need to grieve."

She left with a prescription and a referral. The prescription, she filled. The referral went into the trash. The medication took the edge off. Once the prescription ran out, she began getting this medicine anonymously from multiple sources and had randomly chosen this one as well. LilyQ intrigued her. Unlike the other sources, this one had actually taken the time, insisted actually, that she answered the questions that Lex guessed were to determine if indeed she really needed the medicine. Curiosity kept Lex coming back: Why provide medication illegally and yet ask if she really needed it? Why ask any questions? What was the end game?

In this special forum, privacy and anonymity were as important as the money being exchanged. Still, even the best of them made mistakes and could be traced. Lex would never claim that she was the best; there was always risk. Anyone on the other side might not be safe. There were so many amateurs: wannabe hackers unaware of what was really going on in this arena. This was a place of exchange at a much deeper and often dangerous level.

This psychiatrist, who probably wasn't a psychiatrist, had a security profile that was on par with some of the best of them. That was the draw. There was no reason for someone to have that kind of security in place only to what, provide therapy? No, it had to be more. She wanted to figure out what this person wanted. Because there was always something.

"How many are you taking?" LilyQ inquired.

"A couple a day, plus the morning one," she answered. The questions continued:

"Why the increase?"

"I don't know."

"What's changed?"

"Are you going to send me the meds or what?" Lex asked as she tossed the ball with the dog.

"Humor me," LilyQ typed.

"Fine," Lex replied.

LilyQ continued: "What's changed?"

Lex thought about that for a few seconds before typing:

"I'm bored."

The statement was met with silence, and instead, two question marks appeared.

"Seriously," Lex added.

Again, question marks.

Lex sighed, then typed:

"My brain won't shut up."

"What is it saying?"

"Amusing," Lex said sarcastically.

"What is it saying?"

"Nothing," Lex wrote. "Everything. Like every thought you could ever have, every memory swirling in a vortex."

"And?" LilyQ asked.

Lex stared at the screen.

"I can't stop it or get away from it. It makes me feel like I'm having a heart attack. The medicine makes it bearable, I guess."

"It's a Band-aid," the voice offered.

"What does that mean?" Lex said out loud as LilyQ typed:

"If you need to increase the meds for the same effect, then you aren't healing, you are just putting on a Band-aid."

"Are you going to send me what I need, or do I need to get it somewhere else?" Lex typed.

"You can do whatever you want," was the response.

The exchange continued:

"I'm paying a lot of money for this, what is the big deal?"

"Sometimes it isn't about money."

"What do you want from me?" Lex typed.

"I want to help you," LilyQ responded.

"Why?"

"Because I think I can," the voice responded, "Think about it. Your meds are on the way."

"Thank you," Lex said, adding, "maybe next time you can tell me what you want."

"You are welcome."

Lex closed the link and clicked on a name: Charles Theirry.

"Hmm. What did you do, to make someone mad enough to be here?"

She knew it was irrelevant. Whatever it was, it wasn't interesting. Even this no longer occupied the constant swirl in her brain. Wherever she ran, it was never far enough.

'..you can't go on thinking nothing's wrong...' The Cars

Across town, Allison sat at her kitchen table moving the half-eaten food around her plate. She stared absently at the clock, listening to the second hand tick. From the bedroom, she could hear her husband trying to reason with his four-year-old about how many stories he would read to her before she had to go to sleep, and this made her laugh to herself. Avery completely owned the conversation and was strategically waging psychological warfare to get an extra five minutes.

'How could he refuse?' she thought, knowing that she too, in spite of knowing exactly what the girl was doing, almost always gave in. It was only Aiden's mother that had any resistance to the girl, and she was thankful that someone had taught the child some boundaries.

Finally, Aiden rejoined her at the table and noticing the mutilated food, asked:

"What's up?"

"I was just thinking about us, about Avery, about how us getting married affects her," Allison replied.

Aiden kissed the top of her head before sitting.

"Go on," he said.

"We have to be careful, Aiden. What if it's too soon for me to adopt her? Avery is so sweet and vulnerable, and me coming into her life..."

"...is the best thing that I could hope for," Aiden said, adding, "and, it's a little late in the process to just be bringing this up. It's tomorrow."

Allison continued, "I know. I'm a little nervous...you heard your mom. Avery started crying at the prospect of me being her mom and then me dying."

"She's a little girl, isn't that what children do?" he asked.

"Sure," she responded. "Look, I'm not saying there is anything wrong or abnormal, I just want us to be mindful that she has thought about it and that it obviously affected her..."

"...and Mom handled it fine, Allison," he interrupted.

"She told her I wouldn't die."

"I think you are overthinking it," Aiden responded cautiously. "What is your concern?"

"What if I die?" she asked him.

Aiden laughed.

"I'm serious, Aiden. What if I die, and we let her believe that I will never leave? How would she trust you or your mother or anyone? She will think I don't love her."

"Then we'll get her a goldfish," he replied.

"Wow. You would replace me with a goldfish," Allison said, knowing that this was uncomfortable for him, but annoyed nonetheless.

Aiden chuckled, but seeing that she was frustrated, quickly recovered:

"No, I meant we can get her a goldfish, and when it dies, which will probably be very quickly because I have a bad fish reputation, we will explain to her that love doesn't die."

"You know it doesn't work like that," Allison stated seriously.

"Look, we're fine," Aiden said sincerely. "You love her and don't want her to get hurt. I love that about you."

"What did you tell her about her mother?" Allison asked bluntly. Normally, she let Aiden bring up his late wife when he was comfortable, but the question had been on her mind for some time, and this seemed as good of a time, not that there was one, to ask.

Aiden stopped smiling and looked away nervously. Allison continued:

"I know it's a sore topic, but I really want to know because Avery, as smart as she is, never says anything to match what you just said about love never dying. She shows me pictures of her Grandmother and says she is in heaven watching her but nothing about her mother."

Aiden sighed before speaking:

"When she was old enough to understand that she didn't have a mom, we told her that her mom got sick and died."

"That's it?" This was not the response she expected.

"Look, I was angry, ok? I didn't want to tell my daughter that her mother loved her and was in heaven or any of that nonsense. And Mom agreed because one day, Avery will know the truth about her mother. So, you tell me, what would I say to her then if I let her believe that her mother loved her and just died and then boom 'by the way, your mother killed herself'?"

"Aiden, I'm not trying to argue with you," Allison stated.

"Then what?" he said, not wanting to have this conversation.

"Does she even think that her mother loved her?" Allison asked sincerely.

"She's four," he replied.

"Yes," Allison continued, "she knows you love her, Lex loves her. Lilah loved her."

Aiden took a deep breath before responding coldly:

"Melissa didn't love her."

"You know what?" Allison responded, taking her plate to the sink, "I'm sorry. I know this is a touchy subject. I wasn't there. I just need to understand, I guess..."

Aiden came up behind her, wrapping his arms around her waist and kissing her gently on the side of her neck, causing Allison to smile in spite of herself.

"You know," she told him, turning to look into his eyes, "that won't always work with me."

"Noted," he said. "I will take advantage, then, while it still does."

7

The Los Angeles traffic on the 10 was stop and go, nothing unanticipated; however, Lex wasn't used to riding in the back seat, and the steady jolt was making her nauseous. She made a mental note to insist on driving in the future. Avery chattered away next to her, which left Lex unusually irritated. The sound, any sound, was keeping her from focusing on not vomiting. Avery's voice, along with the radio and Aiden and Allison's conversation crowded her brain. Lex cracked the window and rested her head against it. She closed her eyes, trying to lose herself in the calm rhythm of Trevor Hall's voice through the radio in the background behind the voices in the car.

Adoption day, 10 a.m. Even though they were married and, legally, Allison was Avery's stepmother, Aiden wanted it to be more. Perhaps it was his way of trying to completely erase Melissa. Or maybe this was just about moving on. Was this a good idea? Lex wasn't certain. It made Aiden content, and Avery was excited. But Avery was four years old. Her thoughts were focused on having a mommy. She had no way of understanding that Allison was easily already her mother without the formality of adoption. The way they had explained it to her was simplified: We are going to a special place where special people would say 'Do you want Allison to be your Mommy?' and if she said yes, then poof, Allison would be her real mommy.

Lex felt like all of this was a bit fast; they had only been married a few months. But this was not her decision to make, and the spark in her son's eyes whenever Allison entered a room was vastly different from the infatuation from his early days with Melissa. That look, the calm, it was everything she hoped for him, so what could she do but agree and support them?

This, though...this made her uneasy. It would mean that legally Allison could make decisions for Avery, take her anywhere. She would have more right to her than Lex. Once Melissa was gone, Lex never contemplated anyone taking her place. Sure, she knew that Aiden would probably find someone new, but Lex always thought that, in a way, she would be the one to ultimately have the say over Avery's life decisions. It was selfish, she knew, and irrational.

'And controlling.'

Allison was a wonderful person, but Lex worried.

'What if she is a bad mother? What if she and Aiden didn't stay together? How would she be able to control...'

That is as far as the thought ever went. Lex knew better than to let herself go down an irrational path.

'*You agreed to this,*' her conscience, now equipped with Lilah's voice, reminded her in her head.

When they discussed this with her before they were married, she sucked down her fears and said that it was a great idea. Of course, that was because they weren't married, and she didn't think it would happen so quickly. That Allison took her aside quietly and asked her how she felt about it, that she said her opinion was important to her, seemed sincere. They were both clear that her permission wasn't necessary, but it felt respectful and at least well played; Allison understood Lex's influence. She just hoped she wouldn't regret agreeing, well, hoped that Allison didn't regret it. And being honest with herself, Lex owed Avery and Aiden her support. Maybe that would count somewhere down the road.

Aiden pulled into the courthouse parking garage. He made his way floor by floor, looking for a parking space.

"Jesus, this place is a nightmare," he commented out loud.

Only something this important, or jury duty, would bring him anywhere close to the downtown area in the middle of the morning traffic.

"There," Allison pointed to an empty space as they almost passed it by.

He backed into the spot and quickly got out of the car.

"Come on, we're going to be late!" he exclaimed.

"Relax," both Lex and Allison said in unison and then laughed.

"Seriously, I didn't plan to be sitting behind an accident for half an hour," he complained as he unbuckled Avery from her booster seat and scooped her into his arms.

Allison's phone rang. She looked down at it nervously.

"I'm sorry, babe," she said, without even looking at him, "I have to take this, really quick, I swear."

Aiden rolled his eyes but nodded. He had grown accustomed to random calls from patients or the on-call service. He had no room to complain, he had his share.

The scene playing out before her reminded Lex so much of herself and Lilah, she the eye roller always in a hurry and Lilah relaxed and confident that time was not the enemy and that the world wouldn't end if they were late.

"Go on ahead," Lex told him, shooing him away from the car, "we'll catch up."

"Ok. Just...never mind. Fifth floor, room D," he told Lex.

"Got it, son," she told him.

Lex tried to block out Allison's one-sided call while using the visor mirror to put her hair up and fix her makeup.

'Not too bad,' she thought. A tired woman stared back at her, but otherwise, she was rather well put together for court and what she assumed would be at least one picture. She listened to Allison's conversation without giving it much thought.

"...keep her on suicide watch and up the sedative. I will do the intake evaluation tonight. Yes. Thank you."

Allison ended the call, dropping her phone into her bag.

"Ok, ready?" she said.

"I think Aiden was less nervous when we got married," Allison shared as they walked to the elevator.

'So nervous he asked where the rings were every five minutes,' Lex thought as they stepped into the elevator.

"How do you do that?" Lex asked her.

"What?" Allison replied.

"How do you just turn it off?"

Allison pushed '5' in the elevator and replied:

"It's hard sometimes, especially with patients I have built a relationship with. I have to compartmentalize the work...turn off the office light and shut the door, so to speak. I wouldn't be effective if I couldn't separate the two..."

The elevator jolted and stopped, and they were in blackness. Seconds later, a different, dimmer light came on. Outside, they could hear the shrill bell alarm. Instinctively, Lex hit the 5 button repeatedly and, realizing they were not moving, pushed the emergency button.

"God dammit. Hello?" she said into the speaker.

"Hello, ma'am. I apologize, we've had a slight issue. How many people are in this car?" The voice was fuzzy but audible. She answered him:

"Two of us. Can't you open the door manually? We're going to be late..."

"Sorry, ma'am," he replied, "you are between floors. You'd only be staring at a brick wall. Hang tight. And don't worry, we're just waiting for instruction, and we'll get you moving. Where are you headed?"

"Adoption proceeding, fifth floor, room D. Aiden and Allison Vance. The mom is with me. My son is going to be really upset if..."

The voice interrupted:

"We'll let them know. Hang tight. This should only take a couple minutes."

Lex turned, "I can just hear Aiden now..." She stopped.

Allison was huddled in the corner, her head down, arms wrapped around her knees. She looked like a small, frightened child.

"Alice? Hey, what's going on?" Lex said calmly.

Allison was pale and shaking.

"I can't do this...we have to get out of here. I can't breathe," she responded quietly.

As Lex eased closer, she began to say "They're working on it..." but was abruptly cut off by Allison's panicked voice:

"No. I have to get out of here!! I can't...I just can't."

Lex was completely out of her element and taken back by Allison's reaction.

'What's this about?' she thought but didn't say, worried that she might make it worse.

Lex thought back to when Aiden was a child and something frightened him. She approached Allison slowly and bent down to her level.

"Allison?" she said softly, putting her hand gently on her knee. "Alice," she began. Allison seemed to be somewhere else.

"Alice...Allison, look at me," she said sternly, finally capturing her gaze. She continued quietly, "It's ok, you are ok. Just breathe."

Allison nodded, taking a deep breath, then another, and instinctively Lex sat down next to her and pulled her closer. She stroked her hair for a few moments until she felt Allison's grip loosen a bit.

"Sorry," she said. "Some psychiatrist I am, huh?"

Lex chuckled, "Well...what was that about compartmentalizing?" She could tell the girl was still terrified.

Her curiosity was killing her, but that was for another day.

'Distract her,' she told herself.

"Maybe don't see patients in small spaces?" she offered.

Allison rubbed her forehead, still unfocused.

"Hey, did Aiden ever tell you why he became a doctor?" Lex asked the traumatized young woman.

Allison shook her head no.

"Well," Lex began, "much of who he is, he is because of his Grandfather..."

Six months into her relationship with Lilah, too soon, she remembered complaining, Lilah begged her to meet her father. With Lilah's mother deceased, it was Al that she always confided in, shared her life with, and he wanted to meet her. So reluctantly, they planned dinner at his house.

"My dad is a fabulous cook," Lilah told her.

Lex was nervous. What if she said something stupid? Was he even ok with his daughter dating a girl? What if he didn't like her? But she wasn't nervous for long.

"Lilah!" he exclaimed from the doorway, pulling her into an embrace.

"Hey," she replied.

He was a thin man, clean shaven with dirty-blond and grey peppered hair. Long hair. Gathered at his neck into a rubber band. He was dressed in jeans and was wearing a short-sleeved button up, the kind retired men in Miami wore.

"And you are Alexis." To Lex's shock, and discomfort, he grabbed her into a hug. "Nice to meet you."

"Pop!" Lilah scolded, and he let her go.

"Call me Al," he said as Lex stood staring at him in awkward silence. "Well then, come on in."

"Al" wasn't anything like she imagined. He was an aging hippie, and Lilah was so...not.

"Not what you pictured, hmm?" he asked her later when Lilah excused herself to make a call.

The observation made her laugh, and she replied, "No, definitely not."

He pulled out a joint and lit it.

"Yeah, well, I guess she had to rebel somehow. All that professional, corporate blah."

He laughed sincerely, offering the joint to Lex. She motioned 'No thanks.'

"She's 'the man,'" he said.

"That she is," Lex agreed. "And you are right, I don't think I could have imagined you."

"Well," he exhaled, "she always liked order, never liked to be dirty. You love her, don't you?"

Lex hadn't even said the word to herself, too afraid to express it, to feel something for anyone. Was it that obvious?

"I do," she heard herself say.

He was a comfortable place. Energetic, charismatic. Easy to be with, to talk to. He always called her Alexis, never Lex or Lexi. She hated that name, but from him, it felt right. In spite of herself, she had great fondness for the man. Theirs was a special relationship: a friend, a father, or at least, what she pictured having a father was supposed to be like.

When their son was born, it was natural to entrust his daycare to Al. Who better to fill his days when work took their time? Who better than the man who gave her Lilah? And so, from his first breath, Aiden Alan and Grandpa Al were best friends.

Lilah insisted that Aiden start preschool when he turned three, and it was a toss-up as to who cried more that first day. As Aiden grew, Lex was relieved to find that he was more like him than her in spite of genetics; she was so scared that anyone with her genes would be screwed up, so much so that she almost refused to have a child.

Al was diagnosed with cancer the year Aiden turned fourteen. When he died, part of Aiden's soul went with him. But Grandpa Al told him to live and laugh. Grandpa Al taught him to respect and take care of all creatures, and they were often bandaging some small animal they found in the woods or on the street. Aiden wanted to save the world. And that was all Al.

"For that, I am forever grateful," she told Allison.

"I've seen his picture," Allison said quietly. "It's nice to add dimension to it."

She had stopped shaking, and the color had returned to her face.

"He was the finest man I ever met," Lex offered honestly, and for a few minutes, they sat in vulnerable silence, neither feeling completely comfortable or sure what to say. Finally, the regular overhead lights flickered, and Lex helped Allison stand up as the elevator gave a slight jolt and then began moving. Lex squeezed her hand once more before letting it go. The door opened.

"Are you ok?" Aiden asked, grabbing Allison into an embrace. It was obvious to Lex that he had already known she would be distressed.

"Of course," Lex offered quickly without missing a beat, "why wouldn't she be? C'mon."

She grabbed Avery's hand, and catching Allison's eyes with a knowing look, she added, "We've waited long enough for a mommy already."

"Yeah," the little girl agreed.

That day, Aiden and Avery truly seemed whole for the first time since...everything. Lex pondered this while she tried to find the calm that would let sleep take her. All that she promised Lilah was made good with a few words, the tap of a gavel (that the judge invited Avery to do) and the signing of documents. Aiden and Avery were ok, and she had nothing to do with it; this was all organic and all Allison. It should have felt good; it should have brought Lex some peace when she finally slept. It did not.

The dream was winter dark. Lexi was standing in her living room, suddenly conscious. She could feel her sister and knew that she was somewhere in the house. Looking around at that black furniture, the red carpet, she felt a bit shocked. And curious.

She could feel herself fading away, becoming a kid again, and it scared her. It made her feel vulnerable. She ran for the stairs. In her room, she would be safe, but she got stuck halfway up the stairs. In fact, her legs wouldn't move past the third stair. It was like quicksand, and she backed down, going instead into the basement and into her sister's room.

Her messy twin bed, the second bed to their once shared bunk beds, faced the window. Her stuffed animals were everywhere. Daylight peaked through the window just under one side of the curtains. The window was high; a basement window at ground level in a room mostly underground. It was a shelter...and a tomb.

Lexi turned to look at the velvet clown painting that hung next to the bed so that she could check to see if today the clown's gloved hands looked like gloves or claws. The picture was missing.

Her sister's room was small, the walls covered in thin paneling from the seventies. The added rectangle closet took up even more of the small space, and it stuck out almost to the side of her bed. Lexi was losing herself. She could feel what remained of the strong rational adult melting away from the top down, like the feeling of quickly drinking a cold glass of water on a very hot day; the way the cold liquid runs down into the stomach, only this was a coldness from the head down to the feet. It was startling. It was numb and hopeless.

The closet. It looked empty and hazy. The smell of wet mildew filled the air. Lexi knew the clown was there, and he faded in, looking more like a homeless ragged creature than a man. There was no sound, and honestly, she was not afraid of him; she was used to him.

He was always either unhappy or scary, and today he was unhappy. His clown paint was faded and peeling. He was an old, weathered man. He opened his mouth wide, exposing sharp, rotting teeth. They stared at each other. Really, she was staring at his mouth: open, straining and screaming with no sound.

From his jawline back, the paint and the skin melted, first a slow drip, then running down the neck like candle wax. It was bloody and smooth, and she could feel the warmth of the melting. Quickly, there was just exposed pink and white bone, teeth still in as the decay started to take over the rest of his face. He turned slowly away and faded into the haze, still silently screaming...

The dreams had been coming with more intensity. Sometimes, Lex could simply turn on the light and walk around for a few minutes and the panic would subside. Sometimes she could barely get to the medicine cabinet to take the Ativan that was supposed to calm her. This was one of those times, and she found the best she could do was sit down on the cool kitchen tile with her back against the wall and her head resting on her knees. These were anxiety attacks, she knew this, but it still felt like she was going to die. Her heart pounded against her chest. It hurt. Her arms were numb and tingling. She couldn't breathe.

The dog had followed her. He stretched and yawned and then sat staring at her, whining. When she didn't respond, he disappeared and then returned with a ball, which he dropped at her feet and stood wagging his tail.

'Fricken dog,' she thought, *'I'm dying, but hey, the ball still needs to be thrown, right?'*

Lex could barely catch her breath, but she threw the ball anyway, and the dog took off after it. It made her smile. This was their routine, and it helped her refocus. Once the attack subsided, she changed out of the sweat soaked pajamas, got the dog a treat, took an Ativan, and went back to bed, lights and TV on. The attacks drained her physically and emotionally, yet they caused fierce insomnia, in spite of the medication.

She stared at the TV screen. LilyQ was now a two-dimensional character, a cartoon not yet completely formed. A blank avatar. As an experiment, Lex was letting the program decide what the character would look like...if she even continued to communicate with this person. The program was built to evolve over time based on the conversations. It would analyze the grammar and punctuation, the educational level of the words and phrases, and it would decide what the creature would become. It was designed that way really for Avery so that as she advanced, her characters would advance with her. Right now, Avery's characters always looked like crayon drawings.

"Is there something stronger?" Lex asked.

"Yes, but I don't recommend it," LilyQ's computerized voice said.

"You're not the one dying," Lex told her.

"You're not the one dying either. The clown, though..." LilyQ commented.

Lex instantly regretted saying anything. The synthe-sized voice was a bit eerie, especially when trying to be funny.

"Do you actually help people? Because I'm not feeling it," she said finally.

"Not always," LilyQ responded. "I would like to help you, but you have to participate."

Lex knew damn well what therapy was and what was expected of her. What it had done for her was to allow her to figure out how to get in people's heads, push the right buttons to get them to talk or do things. She wasn't too eager to be on this side of it. She felt resigned that there would never be any peace. She only had that with Lilah.

"Hello?" LilyQ called out, and Lex responded finally:

"I just want to keep it together and not implode. Be-sides, it would be very...identifying to tell you things. You know, dark web for a reason, right?"

"Unless you are that famous and identifiable, I cannot imagine that I could possibly know who you are. I don't need to know who you are," LilyQ answered.

"What do you want from me?" Lex asked again, as she always did.

The avatar stood silent, and Lex elaborated:

"I know there is something. There is always something. I'm going to keep asking, so what do you want?"

"I don't know yet," LilyQ responded. "When I know, I will ask."

"Finally," Lex said, relieved that they were being honest. "Thank you. What if I don't want to give you what you want?"

"I won't ask for anything that you are not willing to provide," was the response.

"That makes no sense but fair enough. Meanwhile, what do I do to not die?" Lex asked.

LilyQ responded, "Tell me what you need."

"I don't want to implode," she restated. "I have responsibilities and until those end, I need to be a bit more than nominally functional."

"Yes, you have said what you don't want. But what do you need?" LilyQ asked again.

"I don't know," Lex answered honestly.

"So that would be something to think about. It is helpful to have a goal that means something to you," LilyQ explained.

Lex stared at the screen.

'What do you mean, what do I need? I need my life the way it was before,' she thought.

"What I need is irrelevant," she began, "What I want is to take a bath without the desire to hold a razor blade against my skin. What I want is to survive until I no longer have to be responsible."

"When is that? Do you have a timeline?" LilyQ asked her.

Lex pondered the question before responding, "I'm not sure. Why would you ask that?"

LilyQ explained her inquiry: "Full disclosure. I can't see you or hear your real voice, so I can only assess where you are in your head by asking you if you have a plan. A timeline to your own self-destruction."

That made sense.

"Well, I'm not there yet," Lex stated honestly.

"I'm glad to hear it. Also, I am asking for you to commit to reaching out if you ever feel like you are going to kill yourself. I would like the respect from you to have an opportunity to address it before you might do something," LilyQ told her.

"Sure," Lex agreed easily. It made no difference to her, this perceived commitment, especially coming from a computerized voice.

Her computer beeped its random new target choice that Lex had searched for to fill the widening void. She was feeling a bit uncomfortable and even a bit exposed, and she hadn't even said anything yet.

"I've got to go," Lex typed, instead of speaking.

Taking a prompt from Lex, LilyQ typed: "Message me when you want to talk. If I am not on, leave me a time, and I will respond."

Lex closed the window and read the details of the person in front of her.

'Blah blah disappear...proof for insurance...'

She clicked it away. Even she had limitations. This wasn't a moral thing, it was a risk thing. Insurance companies were ruthless investigators, and their cyberspace was extremely well guarded. Lex knew this because she helped design just one of the many layers of security that many companies used. Besides that, most people looking to cash in were stupid, they always got caught, and they always talked.

'What do I need really?' she thought.

'Nothingness,' the voice in her head answered back.

A cold sensation ran down through her.

8

The heat of the August sun baked through the ever-present layer of smog, amplifying its intensity. Even in the shade with the cooling mist on high, it seemed unbearable to be outdoors. Despite this, Lex's backyard was alive with music, conversation, and the sound of people splashing in the pool. This had been a constant for many years. There were always events, birthdays, holidays, always planned by Lilah, which Lex realized after she died, and this was the first time since Lilah's last birthday that there were more than five people together in her home at one time. Admittedly, Lex realized that she both missed and hated the chaos. In fact, she had become quite isolated over the years.

"Mom, I really want to do my birthday at the house, the way we used to," Aiden had told her. "The guys haven't seen you in ages. They miss you. C'mon, it will be fun."

Their home had been a second home to most of Aiden's friends growing up. Everyone was now in her backyard: the friends Aiden grew up with along with the friends and colleagues of his and Allison's from work, and their children.

"Mom," one of the guys, Steven, called out to her, "come outside with us!"

"In a minute," she called back.

It was nice to just stand and watch them all like it was before when she and Lilah were simply referred to collectively as 'Moms.' She pictured Lilah making the rounds, always asking if anyone needed anything. She would be wearing a bathing suit, probably blue, with a sarong wrapped at the waist. Her sunglasses, meant to shade her eyes from the glaring sun, would always be on top of her head.

A loud splash brought her back to the present.

"Lilah," she said with a sigh.

Before heading out, she grabbed the mail from the front, noticing a somewhat familiar looking man parked in a car across the street. She couldn't quite place him and was going to ask Aiden who he was, but he drove away before she could make any connection. It really had been a while, maybe too long. She and Lilah always made a point to meet everyone and worked together to actually remember them, their kids, the conversations. Lex had a lot of catching up to do. She caught Aiden several times throughout the afternoon to ask:

"Who is that lady over there, the one in red. Do I know her?"

"I don't think so. That's Dr. Lane. Stacey. She's a surgeon," he responded.

"Who's the guy with the white Nissan who left early?"

"I don't know, Mom, a lot of people have come and gone," Aiden told her finally, "Go on and talk to people, they all know who you are; seriously, everyone has wanted to see you or meet you for a long time. Just have fun."

As the day wore on, Lex remembered why they did this: It was nice to be surrounded by life, nice to hear people enjoying themselves, even if she herself found it hard to feel really engaged. She kept waiting to hear Lilah's laugh, to see her hover around the BBQ, to finally sit down with her towards the end of an afternoon, exhausted from entertaining. She missed sitting out by the pool with her on warm summer nights, sometimes talking about the day, sometimes sitting in silence with just the sound of the jacuzzi overflowing into the pool.

By early evening, "life" began to overwhelm her, and Lex excused herself. There had been enough nice today and more than enough missing Lilah.

"Lex?" she heard at her bedroom door. It was late, she must have fallen asleep.

It was Allison. She looked tired.

"Come in," she told her, then asked, "You ok?"

"Yes," Allison replied, "A lot of people, a lot of hours. I'm not used to it, I guess."

"Me either. Well, not now anyway," Lex told her, motioning for her to sit on the bed as she spoke:

"We used to do this all the time. Lilah loved it."

"We never did this," Allison commented absently, "I always feel a bit out of my league."

"Really? You seemed to fit right in," Lex observed.

"That's nice of you to say. I'm just not used to this. So much chit-chat. Besides, people tend to act a lot different when they find out what I do," Allison shared.

"I guess you are used to more in-depth conversations?" Lex asked her.

"You would think so, though, actually there is a lot of silence and denial. And psychosis."

The young woman's matter of fact answer made Lex laugh.

"Well, you pull it off nicely. Are you guys heading out?" she asked.

"Yes," Allison answered with a laugh, "Avery put herself to bed a while ago, ok if we leave her?"

Lex nodded her approval.

"We'll be back in the morning to clean up anyway," Allison commented, then asked hesitantly, "I've been wanting to ask, how is the anxiety?"

"I'm good," Lex lied.

"Are you sleeping ok?" Allison continued.

"I sleep." Lex couldn't decide if she was annoyed. "Alice, I really don't want to have a discussion with you about my mental health."

"Fair enough," Allison replied, "but I'm not asking like a shrink, I'm asking because we are family."

"Point taken. Look, it's not you, I swear. I just don't trust psychiatry," Lex admitted.

"Got it," Allison said, starting to stand.

Instinctively, Lex reached out but held back from grabbing her arm. Though it wasn't her intent, she knew she hurt the young woman's feelings.

"Alice..." she began.

Allison cut her off, "You know, I really don't trust parents any more than you trust psychiatrists. It's not like I have much experience in a family. I don't always know where I am crossing the line. Sometimes I think I am better at being a psychiatrist than a person."

The statement caused Lex to want to laugh again; however, seeing Allison's expression, and realizing she was dead serious, she held back, speaking instead:

"You didn't...it's reasonable, what you asked. I am watching Avery, and you have a right to know if she's safe." Lex chuckled in spite of herself, "I'm just not reasonable...or normal."

She sighed and continued, "Lilah was reasonable...and normal where it counted."

"I hear a lot about Lilah, and I imagine she was a wonderful woman," Allison replied, "and maybe you could argue that she was what you're not. But Aiden lost a wife and mother in the same month and was left with an infant to raise in a hectic career. And here he is, so calm, so normal, and Avery is so incredibly smart and well adjusted. That's to your credit."

"Maybe. Anyway...this is where we are. I guess we'll have to figure it out as we go along. Keep saying what's on your mind. Right?" Lex asked.

Allison nodded, and Lex hugged her lightly, offering:

"Alice, I'm your mom now. I think you just need to decide what that means for you as much as I do. And sometimes, being a person sucks."

"Thanks," Allison told her. "I know. Maybe I just needed to hear it."

'She is so much like me.' Lex thought as Allison walked away. *'I'm not sure that is such a good thing.'*

Separating Alice, the daughter, from Allison, the psychiatrist, was challenging. The first psychiatrist Lex had interacted with was a creepy, overly affectionate man, a friend of the family. He used his knowledge of human nature to manipulate the people around him. He slept with his patients. His kids were both addicted to prescription medication, and his wife was a shell of a person who, one night while he showered, took out his gun and blew her brains out. And that was the first of many bad experiences that left Lex insecure with any type of personal questions. She wanted to share that with Allison, that her hesitance had nothing to do with her, but she didn't: because she wanted to share it. And not understanding why she wanted to share such a personal detail kept her silent.

Across town that evening, Jacob Staley sat in his Inglewood motel room looking through images on his cellphone. It had been a challenge to find her. There was very little information and a few years' distance, but there she was. He stopped on a picture of Avery. He was sure that was her: Melissa's daughter. She was a clone of Melissa at that age.

The air conditioning unit hanging from the only window sputtered and stopped. Jacob picked up a beer bottle and hurled it at the unit.

"Goddamn stupid...fuck!!" he yelled out.

A month he'd been here, stuck in this crap motel. A month of tracking down his sister. Weeks of confirming she was dead. He assumed this for years, since she didn't show up at his mother's and hadn't written to him or called.

He sat in prison biding time. It was like his sister to up and change her mind, disappearing for ages. In his mind, he hoped that was true, that he'd come out to find her and tell her to come home, that she belonged with him. They were going to be a family again, she had promised him that. She, his mother and the child. A real family this time.

His mother died with Jacob still having another year of his sentence to serve, still believing that she would come home.

"Jake, you're gonna go get them when you get out, right? Bring them back where they belong?" His mother asked this at every visit.

"Yeah, Mom, of course," he told her every time. Including the last time he saw her.

Months it took him to work, nose down, parole meetings kept. Months to procure a new identity, get money. He was sitting here sooner than he planned, but he'd lost his temper and put the woman he was with in the hospital, so he had to move quickly. Luckily for him, she had actual possessions that he could pawn and get the hell out of there.

'We could have had it good,' he thought, remembering his last encounter with the woman and the uncontrollable rage she made him feel.

Why were people always fucking things up for him? What had angered him that time? He couldn't remember. The screaming? Yes. The sound of her face hitting the bathroom mirror and the sound of shattering glass as it fell into the sink and onto the floor and the instant silence that followed as the woman slumped to the floor? Absolutely. The silence of that moment had been comforting, freeing.

He zoomed in the picture of the little girl.

Two things were certain: One was that his sister would never have killed herself as was reported. She knew she didn't have the right. She belonged to him. Two was that he had come for what was his.

'Pretty little thing. Uncle's going to take good care of you.'

9

"I had a way then losing it all on my own..."
-Ellie Goulding

It was just before dawn, and Lex sat curled up on the sofa listening to the birds as they woke, first one, then two and then a chorus singing in the new day at first light. She was chatting with LilyQ, but her thoughts were somewhere else.

"Lexi, look at the guy over there with the bird," Tony's voice haunted from the long ago Hollywood days past.

She stretched and ran her hand through her hair. Too much old stuff was crowding her brain. This was another life, another Lex, dead and buried. There had been so many...

"Lexi, look," Tony insisted.

They had all crowded into a booth at Popeyes, the only place open in Hollywood in the middle of the night, the only place that welcomed anyone. 'They' were a revolving set of non-existent creatures; discarded in one way or another by life, it was always a toss-up who would survive the day and make it back to the night.

The old man in the booth across the way was from head to toe one color: homeless. It was that washed out gray-brown non-color of those people in the background, like the non-color of a war-ravaged city, that gray concrete dust covering everything and all color of life gone. There he sat in the booth with a cup of water and a piece of chicken. On the table in front of him was a knit cap, and cuddled inside was a little bird.

What caught Tony's attention and then all of theirs was that the man was taking tiny pieces of chicken, chewing it up, taking it from his mouth and placing it in the bird's mouth, which the bird seemed to be chewing, or swallowing, whatever birds do. But then, right in front of them, the bird's head fell to the side.

"Man, your bird is dead!" someone from her table called out, though Lex couldn't remember who. The man shook the bird a little, then put his mouth over the bird's beak and tried to breathe into it, and when that didn't work, the man suddenly got up, grabbed the bird and ran out of the restaurant.

At their table, they were all quiet for what seemed like forever until someone said, "What the fuck?" Then, the event erased by that statement, they all went back to their previous conversation, but Lexi just sat there crying silently for the first time in what seemed like a lifetime...

Lex's eyes watered remembering this man, who did not exist except to this bird as he fed it, and then, bird dead, slipped quickly back into non-existence. The TV beeped, and Lex looked up, blinking away tears.

"Do you have any siblings?" appeared in the cloud next to the face of the ever-changing character on the screen.

Lex studied the shape of the partially formed image. Whether or not the person on the other end of the conversation was female or male was not clear, in spite of the moniker LilyQ, but at some point during the interactions, Lex's interpretation had made it female.

"???" popped up on the screen.

She started to type a response then hesitated and turned on the voice-over.

"Yes," she said reluctantly, "a sister."

"Where is she?" LilyQ asked.

"I'm not sure," Lex answered.

"What does that mean?" the computerized voice responded.

Lex ignored the question and returned to typing her response:

"She was cute, always had short hair because when it was long, it was always a matted mess.

'So innocent,' she thought, continuing to type.

"She wanted to be 'the Six Million Dollar Man.'"

"Wasn't there a 'Bionic Woman?'" the voice asked, and Lex typed:

"Yes. She wanted to be a boy when she was little. She was smart, knew what she wanted, that's for sure."

"Care to elaborate?" LilyQ asked, though it seemed more like an order.

"We had these next-door neighbors that were pretty wild. I must have been four when they first existed to me, sitting on the floor of my bedroom with my mother as she explained to me with stick figure drawings how the kids had set fire to an upstairs bedroom...Will, Scott and Angie. They all looked alike, except Will had light brown hair, Scott had stark yellow hair (the same color as his mother had her hair dyed) and Angie had dark brown hair. As children, we thought they were lucky: no real curfew, no rules, they went to school but never worried about grades or tests. They were fearless, godless. As an adult remembering them, I see now that their futures were already visible in their eyes." Lex sighed, adding:

"Anyway, it was what it was."

"What does that mean, they were godless...they didn't go to church? Didn't believe in God?" LilyQ inquired.

"No," Lex answered, "godless, like without having a sense of safety, surviving in a world where you don't exist with value or purpose. Wandering from one moment to the next. Where sense of self isn't nurtured or guided, instead it's a compilation of misguided immature experiences. It makes your soul different, alone."

"Huh. That's an interesting perspective. Tell me the rest," LilyQ said, "you don't say much about yourself as a child."

Lex rubbed the palm of her hand with her thumb. Her wrists started to hurt more quickly these days. It sucked getting older. She continued:

"So, Will was two years older than me, Scott was my age and Angie was my sister's age. They were our friends on and off over the years. Well, maybe not friends, more like acquaintances. Sometimes I hung out with them on summer evenings, and we would catch fireflies and eat blackberries off the wild bushes that grew across the street. After dark, we would sit around and use our half-bitten fingernails to mark X's in mosquito bites to stop them from itching."

As she spoke, Lex felt the vulnerability in saying out loud what was private and hers. It made her feel uncomfortable, reminded her that only Lilah knew her, at least as much as she was willing to let her. It felt like betrayal telling someone else. It felt like betrayal sharing parts of her that she had never shared with Lilah, but she continued...

"Scott and I and his best friend Ty played together at school, mostly superheroes at recess, because during the winter, running around was the only way to keep warm. Ty was my first boyfriend. This was in second grade. His mom sold high-end costume jewelry, and he used to steal rings and give them to me. The best one was silver and had two interlaced open stars on it." Lex smiled at the memory and continued, "I was a jealous girlfriend. He was oblivious to this.

"Every time he spent time with another girl, or we allowed another girl to play with us, I was as bossy and mean as I could be, privately of course, and Scott and Ty were left confused when they would return to our hideout from an adventure and the girl or girls would be gone.

"I didn't care. What's mine is mine, and they were both mine.

"So, this one day, I was playing on the merry-go-round, and one of my friends came up to me to show off the ring that Ty had just given her. It was the same star ring. I was so mad. I was supposed to be special and the only one with a ring."

Lex stopped.

"Why did you stop?" LilyQ inquired.

"This is silly. I was a dumb kid, did stupid things," Lex responded.

"Right," LilyQ agreed, "kids do dumb, immature things. They also act out their own dramas based on what they need or what they are missing."

"None of this really matters now," Lex commented.

"It does. Trust me. Finish the story," the computerized voice said adamantly.

Lex sighed and continued:

"I told her to let me see it. She hesitated but then took it off and handed it to me. I put it on over my mittens and got back on the merry-go-round. She got on after me and someone spun us.

"As we were going around and while she wasn't looking, I took off the ring and threw it, knowing that wherever it landed, it would be in grey slushy snow...very difficult to impossible to find. When the merry-go-round stopped, she asked for her ring.

'Oh no,' I told her, 'it must have flown off. I'm sorry, let me help you find it.'

"It was worth losing the rest of recess 'looking' for the ring.

"The next day, still mad, I told Ty and Scott that I didn't want to play with them anymore. A week later, Ty chased a ball outside of the schoolyard gate and got hit by a car. He spent weeks out of school, and when he returned, I don't think I ever spoke to him again.

"Anyway, since we were next-door neighbors, Scott and I still spent time together. When he wasn't in trouble anyway...I always wondered why kids that had no rules and no curfew were constantly being grounded. But their mom's boyfriend at that time was an angry man. She was gone a lot, and I heard somewhere that he used to like to line them up across the sofa butt naked and whip them with a belt. They never said anything about it. And I never asked.

"I know that almost every time that my sister got permission for Angie to spend the night, something would happen at the last minute to get her grounded, and when we would play dolls with them, I remember that all of Angie's dolls were mutilated, especially the one that was anatomically correct, or at least it was before she bit its penis off. Seriously, the penis was chewed off by human teeth, and their whole house was littered with trash and dirt. I don't believe anyone ever cleaned that house the whole time they lived there. Their mom was really creative, though, and she often tried to pull together some type of club or activity, like 4H.

"One summer, we had this old tent that we put up in the backyard, so she taught us how to make moccasins and Indian Fry bread, and we camped out. She taught us wood carving. The year I was nine...I think, and my sister was seven...she opened a ceramic shop in her garage where anyone could come, pay for a plaster item, then paint it there...obviously ahead of her time since there are shops like that everywhere now.

"She was an artist, I think. She had a summer garden scene with a gazebo painted on her living room wall, and the plaster molded items she had on display were professionally painted with all the extra detail that made them special.

"My mom particularly liked a large red and black painted Spanish Lady and the matching red and black Matador. Our living room back then was furnished red and black...red shag carpet with black leather furniture, so it would have matched perfectly. She talked about buying them for a long time but couldn't afford it, and I really wanted her to have them.

"So, one day while we were playing, Will said, 'If you guys come into the garage and pull down your pants, you can have anything in the shop you want.'

"This transaction seemed reasonable. I thought of this master plan to get one of the pieces my mom wanted. In my head, I pictured just going in, pulling down my pants and then walking in the front door of our house with the Spanish lady for my mom. There was never even a thought that this might be wrong. It just seemed logical.

"Now, my sister and I were always in competition for our mother's praise and attention, and my sister was already headed for the garage while I was still thinking about it, for what I thought was the same idea. The door shut before I even spoke and never mind that I was honestly already thinking of how I was going to convince my sister that this was a good idea: I didn't have to.

"'Wait,' I said. But it was too late.

"She didn't even say if she wanted to or not, she just did it. A few minutes later, she came out with two small plaster items, a mouse and a dog, I think; not something for our mother at all but something she wanted."

"Why didn't you get the Spanish Lady?" was all I could say.

"I don't want that, I want these," she responded, holding up the items.

"Having had the time to think about it, I was going to back out, but since I was the big sister, I really had to go through with it.

"So, I went in.

"The garage was dark except for a stream of light coming from under the garage door. There also would have been light coming from the back door window if Scott wasn't looking through.

"Knock it off," I yelled at him.

Will already had his pants unbuttoned.

"Ok, unbutton yours," he said.

I hesitated.

"Well?" he said.

I unbuttoned my shorts and pulled down the zipper.

"Here, I'll go first," he said and whipped his pants off.

I pulled mine down slowly, never taking my eyes off of his penis.

We stood there for a minute, and then he reached out to touch me. It shocked me, I think, and I reached out and grabbed his penis. He pulled back.

"Hey, I get to touch you, you don't get to touch me," he said loudly.

"No way," I told him.

He got mad and pulled up his pants.

"Take something," he snipped.

I pulled up my shorts and went for the Spanish lady.

He grinned.

"Except that," he said. "That's too big, and my mom will know it's gone."

I ended up picking some random piece off the shelf. I don't even remember what it was. I walked out and across my yard where my mom had come out to call us for dinner.

"Where did you get those?" she asked.

My sister was walking behind me with her treasures.

I started to say that Will gave them to us when I heard him from right behind me.

"My mom said they could have some," he told her straight to her face. "But I don't think she wanted me to give that one away."

He took the plaster figure from my hands and walked away.

My sister smiled and walked past me into the house with her newly acquired treasures, and I just stood there. I guess she knew what the price of the items were, and how much she had to spend.

"Dang," I remember saying out loud. My sister was smart. I never underestimated her after that."

Lex smiled at the thought.

"What did your mom say?" LilyQ asked.

"About what? We didn't tell her anything," Lex responded.

"Why not?" The voice, though computerized, seemed surprised.

"Didn't think about it, I guess. Why would we do that?" Lex asked genuinely.

LilyQ answered: "You don't think that was wrong? That this boy would ask you to take off your clothes and touch you?"

"Well, we did it willingly," Lex offered, "We were all just screwed up kids."

"Yes," the character agreed, but added, "but do you think that was normal behavior? Do you think it was wrong?"

The conversation was giving Lex a headache. She was beginning to regret saying anything. This was exactly why she kept everything to herself, why she shared so little with Lilah, who at least never asked questions, just said, "I love you," or "Your life was crazy, I'm so glad it isn't now."

"Are you still there?" the voice startled her. How long had she been silent? She answered:

"Do I think it was wrong? Now, yes, then...then it was a means to an end. And I learned a lot. Like get paid first," Lex chuckled, "and that my sister was a lot smarter than I gave her credit for."

"What is your sister's name?" LilyQ asked.

"No," Lex said adamantly, "that's mine. I'm not telling you."

"Ok," the voice replied quickly.

"Telling you this doesn't make me feel better," Lex told 'her.'

"How does it feel?" was the response.

Lex answered honestly, "I feel the same, and it feels like nothing. I don't feel anything about it, except irritated."

"Irritated by what you shared or irritated by me?" LilyQ asked her.

"Both," Lex answered, adding, almost in a whisper, "'*Daniel Striped Tiger*' wouldn't keep asking me questions."

"Who?" LilyQ asked.

"Never mind," she replied, deciding it was irrelevant to explain.

"It takes time," the voice offered.

"This is why I hate...this, or talking about myself," Lex shot back.

"Yet here you are."

Lex sighed and agreed: "True that."

"So, how does it feel to talk about that?" LilyQ's continued questions were making Lex question her obsessive need to figure her out, and she answered:

"I already told you."

"No," LilyQ said without missing a beat, "you said it doesn't make you feel better, not how you feel. What does nothing feel like?"

Nothing felt cold, it felt alone. It was a spiraling tunnel of nothingness.

"I don't know," Lex lied.

"So, think about that," typed across the floating text box. "Figure it out and let me know next time. If you figure it out."

"Sure," Lex replied, then asked, "Have you figured out what you want yet?"

The word 'maybe' typed in the text box, followed by 'I'll let you know.'

10

"Gramma, can I get these grape popsicles?"

Avery held them up in front of her. Lex was beginning to regret letting her out of the grocery cart.

"No, Avery," she responded, and still the child kept asking:

"Can I get these red ones?"

"No."

Lex sighed. Shopping with the child was challenging and not at all optimal. If she hadn't lost track of time online, this would have already been done. She made a mental note to set an alarm prior to logging onto or watching anything and laughed to herself. She was running out of ringtones for everything she had on an alarm: Take meds, brush teeth, brush hair. Take meds, do laundry, eat something. Take meds, shower, breathe. Avery today...

Ok, so there were some exceptions. Lex never needed an alarm when Avery was actually with her. Never for feeding the dog, his life was too reactive. And she never forgot to get her nails done; as a child and well into adulthood, her nails were non-existent, chewed down the nail bed. But once she got that under control and her nails grew out, they were always perfect and colored and almost always, her ring finger a different color.

Avery continued her plea:

"The blue ones?"

"Avery, I said no. You have popsicles at home," Lex told her.

Jacob watched the exchange from the end of the grocery store aisle. For days, he had stalked them carefully, looking for a routine. Anger boiled in his stomach, but he remained calm, focusing on Melissa's phone call when she first reached out to him:

"Jacob."

The sound of her voice over the prison phone was a bit hollow and ghostly and he felt instantly haunted. It caused his heart to beat faster and yet soothed him at the same time. He said nothing, opting to hear the sound of Melissa's breathing.

"Jacob?" she said again, this time with hesitance.

To Jacob it sounded desperate and he felt a sense of control wash over him for the first time in years. After all, Melissa had reached out to him, as he knew she would. This made Jacob feel better than he imagined it would and he let the silence linger, knowing that she could hear him breathe, confident that she wouldn't hang up.

"What do you want?" he asked finally, the anger in his voice surprising him a little.

"I...I missed you is all," Melissa responded. She sounded fearful to him.

'*Good*,' he thought.

He had meant for her to suffer for all the time that had passed, while he sat there in prison, and yet minutes later he found himself hypnotized by her voice, her words. How could he stay angry when she was so sorry for leaving him behind? How could he not forgive her this mistake? Instead, he refocused the anger reserved for Melissa to someone else:

To this woman in front of him now, Alexis Vance, who Melissa had told him had not only taken her child but also made Melissa beg to spend time with her, all over an accident. It was this woman, not the kid's father, that he obsessed over for almost three years, day after day thinking about how he would confront her.

Perhaps he should be grateful, and he was at first, that this woman had made Melissa realize home was better. And perhaps it was this woman's doing that made Melissa so eager to come back to him. But now...

It would have been so easy to just take the child now, in their car in the parking lot. He could wait until Avery was belted into the seat. He could push the woman into the car and beat the crap out of her, then he and Avery would be free. He could do that. But he needed more. He needed her to know that he was in charge, not her... that Melissa was his, not hers to take away, and he would make sure she knew that he was the one taking Avery. He needed her to suffer for ruining his perfect life, before he ended hers. But he also needed it to look random.

He didn't care at all what the child's father thought: Jacob could barely think about him existing. The thought that he had been with his sister, held her naked in his arms, fucked her: It was too much for him to entertain. He would just get to suffer the way he suffered, losing forever what belonged to him. For now, it was the woman he wanted. She was tiny, an easy target. He could feel himself grinning.

As Lex pushed the grocery cart towards the counter, she absently glanced up at the mirror in the corner of the store. Instantly, the back of her neck chilled as she caught a glimpse of the man she thought she had seen in front of her house a week prior. She turned quickly. There was no one there. She searched everywhere in her line of sight, but nothing. Instinctively, she grabbed Avery from the cart, heading out the door, leaving the unpurchased groceries behind.

She scanned the parking lot as she quickly strapped Avery into her seat.

"Gramma, my yellow pony...we forgot my yellow pony!" the child complained loudly.

"We'll get another one," Lex told her absently as a hand touched her shoulder and she jumped back.

"Ma'am, you forgot this," the store clerk said, holding out the pony.

"What!?" Lex asked, startled by the encounter.

"My pony!!" Avery exclaimed, reaching for it.

Lex's heart was pounding in her ears.

"Ma'am, are you ok?" the clerk asked.

"Yes...yes, thank you." Lex barely caught her breath.

"Have a good day," the clerk said before walking away.

"Yea, you too," Lex told him, scanning the parking lot.

She caught a glimpse of the Nissan speeding out of the lot and caught only three characters: G73. But it could have been G78. White plate. It might have been a California plate, but it could have been from another state. Lex cursed herself for not wearing her glasses.

At home, she scanned the DMV database. How many people's lives had she ruined over the past few years? And how few faces to connect that to. She was so cautious. Did she miss something? No one matched the description. She typed the partial plate into a search engine. So many combinations, and though she hoped for a quick result, instant gratification, she knew the search was going to take a while.

'Who are you?' she thought, trying to place the familiar features.

Lex did not believe in coincidence. She was aware that sometimes she was paranoid. More than just sometimes. But this...this was something. As the search ran, a new window popped up. LilyQ. Lex glanced at the time: 3:30 p.m. Avery would wake up from her nap soon.

'Fuck timing,' she thought.

"Hello," Lex typed, switching to voice over with her headset in place.

"Hello," the voice replied.

"You figured out what you want from me," Lex stated. It was a confirmation, not a question, since Lex hadn't reached out to her.

"Yes," LilyQ answered.

"Let's have it then," she said quietly.

"I have a patient who needs to disappear. With children." The statement was stark and matter of fact.

Lex stared at the character, silently admitting to herself that this wasn't what she expected.

"What exactly do you think I do?" she asked impatiently.

"You're on a dark site. You don't want to share your name or even provide an alias, strictly numbers. Whatever you do, it's well-guarded, and I think this is something that you can do. Or this is something you can help facilitate," LilyQ replied.

"I don't make people disappear," Lex stated.

"You could make it happen, though, am I right?" LilyQ responded thoughtfully.

"You're crazy," Lex replied, pacing around the living room as the conversation continued.

"But you could do it."

"May I remind you that you are on the same dark site. There are hundreds of people with listings out there that you can hire for this. Any of them can create a false identity," Lex said.

"I don't know them. I know you..."

"You don't know me," Lex interrupted the voice and, unable to resist, asked, "Why?"

"I can't tell you that."

"I can't do it," Lex stated.

"I believe you can," LilyQ countered.

Lex continued pacing the living room. She wasn't concerned about the request and whether she could do it; she could. She wasn't even afraid of being caught; she was confident of her anonymity. So, what was it then?

"Do you have any idea what is involved in what you are asking? Background information, all documentation, who do they know, who knows they exist, who will ask questions?" Lex asked quietly. If Avery hadn't been asleep, Lex's voice would have been much louder and much more passionate.

"I am aware. What is your hesitation?" came the answer.

'My hesitation is that you are asking me.' she thought, *'My hesitation is that I may have bigger problems right now.'*

Lex responded:

"Most people who choose to disappear change their minds. That is how the people that help them end up getting fucked."

A jpeg file popped up on the screen. Lex opened it. The woman's face was swollen to twice the size it should be, eyes swollen shut, a slash across the cheek through the nose. Chunks of hair from the forehead hairline appeared to have been ripped out. Lex was un-phased by the image.

"No," she said.

"What is your hesitation?" the voice demanded.

"Well, let me ask you this: How many times has your patient returned to the person who did this?" Lex asked.

"Several. She isn't my patient. I thought you should see the serious reality of the request," LilyQ responded.

The request seemed off base, and the growing tightness in Lex's chest throbbed like a silent alarm. She had anticipated the need, a desire, some request of quid pro quo because most relationships were quid pro quo. In fact, anyone she had ever talked to for more than ten minutes online always wanted something. But this request was far beyond 'this for that,' this was the kind of request that required time, a more cultivated and, quite frankly, trusting relationship, if there could ever be such a thing. Who asks a stranger, no, who asks someone that could possibly identify them, for something like this? Regardless, she didn't have the time or energy to be tested. It was just like a shrink, like any other shrink, to pull some mind game bullshit, like a picture of some battered woman would make any difference.

"Are you still there?" LilyQ asked.

Lex stared silently at the character.

"You're angry," she said. "It is not my intention to trick you. This is what I need."

"What kind...are you even a doctor?" Lex inquired, catching and lowering her voice so that she did not wake Avery. "If you wanted to know how I felt about domestic abuse, you should have asked..."

"The kind that wants what is best for my clients," the voice interrupted, "and you're right, this woman will never leave. The client is the woman's sister. She wants to take her nieces and leave the situation. They are three years old and eight months old. I cannot legally advise or advocate this. I would lose my license. Do you understand?"

"And this is what you do instead?" Lex asked. "You don't even know me."

"I have a feeling I can trust you," LilyQ stated.

Jesus,' Lex thought before continuing:

"How will you keep this from coming back on you? You realize that you will be the first person that the police will question."

"No, I won't. I'm just the facilitator. What is your price?" LilyQ answered confidently.

"Fine," Lex said.

'This is what you get, Lex. This is why you don't talk to anyone,' she thought as she grabbed the keyboard and sat down on the sofa. The dog, who had been pacing with her, stopped as well and joined her. Lex scratched his chin, saying out loud, "Little partner in crime."

"What was that?" the computer voice asked.

"Nothing," she responded.

"What is your price?" LilyQ asked again.

"Have you done this before?" Lex typed.

"Not to this extent, but yes, there is a network," typed back across the screen.

"So, what are you, some kind of broker? I don't want anything," Lex said. "Send me what you know."

"You should be paid," the voice echoed.

"No," Lex said, "I don't need money. I have money. Trust me if you want to, which I advise you don't, but I do not know you, and I do not trust you."

"Ok," was the response.

"At least you finally told me what you want," Lex offered.

"It's not like that," LilyQ said. "This is not something I really want. I don't want this for anyone."

"It's fine. It's what I expected," Lex stated matter-of-factly.

"I didn't," LilyQ typed, "not like this."

Lex typed a link.

"Send all of the information here. Our connection through this route will have to end. Understand?" Lex said.

"Yes." LilyQ then added, "Will you reach out when you need to talk?"

'Wow...really,' Lex thought.

"I don't know. I just...I don't know. If I do, this never happened," she warned.

"Of course," the voice said. "Understood. Be careful."

"It's you who needs to be careful," Lex warned.

She ended the connection and wiped out the digital signature.

'Don't do it, Lex,' she heard Lilah's voice in her head as she often did, though what was once a loud, sharp plea at the beginning of all of this was now barely a whisper.

Lex opened the file, ignoring the pictures. There was no need to look at them. It was safer for her, safer for them. The important data was there: First names, ages, hair color, eye color, ethnicity.

"I hope you like rain," she said out loud as she typed, and turning to the dog, she asked, "Thoughts?"

The dog wagged his tail at the sound of her voice.

'Don't do it, Lex.'

That she knew better, that it was Lilah's voice in her head...it didn't matter, Lex couldn't help herself...it was a challenge. She was compelled to do it. Maybe that was why her chest hurt. Maybe that was what she should work on with the shrink. Doing this? It would be a rush: satisfying for a while, then it would fade. Outwardly, consciously, it would be no big deal. But the nightmares would come, the haunting violent memories...that was the price.

11

Jacob Staley had nightmares. His were always of loss: First, the loss of his mother's intimate affection when he was in seventh grade and she got remarried...

"It ain't right now, Jake," she had told him, "I got to take care of your stepdad now, you understand, right?"

Next, the loss of his kid when he was sixteen. Melissa was only thirteen at the time, and there were complications. Not that it mattered...a kid would have just gotten in the way of his insatiable need to be with her. And now, Melissa was gone.

Jacob paced back and forth across the fifteen feet of the hotel room, re-living that first time with her: nine and still playing with dolls, yet he couldn't stop himself, ever. Even at seventeen, when she finally said no, had the audacity to tell him she had a boyfriend. God, how it had angered him. No was not an option. She belonged to him, and he took what was his. He went to prison for it that time, but he didn't care. He knew she would be back. She was everything.

And she was coming back to him. But that bitch stopped her, and the thought of that caused Jacob to put his fist through the tiny mirror hanging over the sink. As he washed the blood off his hand, the anger was seething and loud. He headed out to find someone to make him forget Melissa, if only for a few minutes.

Jacob had made a plan: October 12th. No matter what, that would be the day, his gift to his mother. He just needed to find someone to take care of the kid. He needed a family, and it couldn't come soon enough...

Some time after midnight, just as Jacob finished up with his victim, an alert woke Lex from sleep. She clicked on the results. Rented vehicle, white Nissan. CA G780328. Registered guest, Econo Lodge, five weeks ago. Nothing else. He just appeared on the planet. An alias.

"Who the hell is Eric Matthews?" she said to herself.

She searched on. One way ticket from Maryland...

'Oh, fuck.'

Lex felt the blood leave her face and felt her limbs grow cold and numb.

Melissa, who had faded away so easily: It had been too easy. Lex continued her search and confirmed what she feared: They were not safe.

She should have told Aiden immediately. She should have called the police. She could see clearly that Jacob Staley had skipped out on parole, that he was wanted for an assault. She could have turned him in anonymously. Fingerprints would easily identify him, and he could be on his way out of their lives. She could have done this. She should have done this. But would there be questions? What might he know?

On autopilot, Lex went to the garage for some tools, fighting the panic that threatened to take her over. In her bedroom, hands shaking such that she could barely put on gloves, she unscrewed the earthquake brackets from the dresser and corner curio. She moved them to the center of the room. She pried off the baseboards and rolled back a piece of carpet and padding. Under the padding, the floor was concrete. With a crowbar she lifted a large rectangle block of it, propping it open with an attached metal bar. She pulled back a sheet of plastic, revealing a safe. She opened it.

Organized in the safe, along with several wrapped bundles of cash, were several un-assembled guns hand guns, a rifle. She looked through them and pulled out several small pieces and also some ammunition. She reassembled her room. She assembled the gun. It was a perfect match to the one from Lilah, just not as pretty. She loaded it and shoved it under a mattress. She had no idea what the plan was. Prison for him wouldn't be forever. There would be questions about Melissa. He was a loose end.

There were so many resources out there that Lex could hire to handle this. The problem was that she had never engaged any of them personally. She had always avoided involvement in these types of inquiries, always kept herself removed. This was a line in the sand. This had the highest discovery rate. And being discovered was not an option, because having Jacob Staley killed didn't matter, but her son and Avery finding out that she had indeed killed Melissa; that she could not live with. No, Jacob Staley had to go, and Lex had to figure out how to make that happen on her own.

When Lex finally slept, she dreamt of a funeral. It was Lilah's, it was Melissa's. It was Alan's. They were faceless, the people sitting in the church. They spoke to each other without mouths, cried tears without eyes. Her sister was there; crooked pixie cut and in pajamas. She had a face. She laughed outside on a swing. The clown was pushing her higher and higher. Lex's hands were sticky with blood.

"Gramma, come find me," she heard.

'Avery.'

Lex looked down the church aisle, where Avery was running.

"C'mon, Gramma!"

"Avery, come here now!" she scolded in a panic.

Avery laughed and kept running.

"This isn't a game!" Lex yelled and ran after her.

Avery crawled into the coffin.

"No, Avery, stop!" she scolded.

Lex approached the coffin, afraid to look.

Avery's laughter surrounded her. When she looked down at the coffin, she saw herself.

She woke from the nightmare like a jolt of electricity. There was no hope of sleep now, and she laid awake searching for a solution. How was she going to get all of them away so she could figure out what Jacob Staley wanted, and more importantly, what was she going to do about it? They weren't just going to go on a last-minute random trip, not with work, and certainly Allison wouldn't leave her patients for an unplanned vacation. No. Only one thing would make them drop everything. For her. And it was the last thing she wanted.

Lex cursed this choice she knew she'd have to make. Panic filled her in a way that it hadn't in months.

'What are you going to do, Lex?'

She stared at herself in the bathroom mirror. Her lips were starting to pale and tingle, and sweat was visible on her forehead. Her hands shook as she turned on the cold water.

"Stop it!" she commanded.

She began splashing cold water over her face, and when that didn't stop the panic, she walked out into the backyard, jumped into the pool and held herself under water until her lungs could no longer take the pressure. She could feel her heartbeat in every inch of her body. All the while, the dog ran along the pool's edge, barking and whining.

When she finally came up for air, the dog stopped barking, ran and got his ball and dropped it in the water next to her.

She looked him in the eyes, feeling the panic subside.

"Wow, really?" she told him.

As she dried herself, memories of Lilah swirled in her soul. Lex did not want to go to the condo. That place was Lilah on steroids, and Lex's best memories with her were sealed in time with the shutting of the door of that last plane home. Where they belonged. To go there without her meant being there without her. Sleeping there without her. Watching the sun rise and set without her. And yet, that was the safest temporary solution.

She sighed and picked up the phone.

12

A barely audible chime accompanied by a soft pulsing glow interrupted the silence of early dawn, causing Aiden to turn over and instinctively put his pillow over his head. Consciousness slowly jostled him enough to recognize the tone. Next to him, Allison rolled over and away from the sound.

"Get the phone, it's your mom," she said as she turned.

He fumbled for it, bringing the phone to his ear without lifting his head.

"Yeah, Mom?"

"Sorry, I know it's early."

Her voice was quiet as if that made a difference now that he was awake.

"Listen, you said that whenever I was ready to go to the condo we would go. I'm ready now," she told him.

The urgent tone in her voice and the word 'condo' brought Aiden quickly out of his half slumber, and he sat up.

"Mom? Are you ok? What happened?" he asked.

Aiden's change in tone caught Allison's attention and she, too, sat up.

"Yes, I'm fine," Lex assured, "I want to go to the condo. Is it possible for you guys to go?"

"We could get the time off, I'm sure. When do you want to go?" he inquired.

"Now," she said.

He silently processed his mother's request. She was calm, too calm for a spontaneous request.

"Aiden?" he heard.

"Yea...yes, I'm here. This...I'm just trying to think a minute. Mom, what's happening? Why now?" he asked her.

"I'm just ready to go. I need it to be now. Right now, or as soon as right now can be. Please? It's nice there now. Less crowded, and I can get a really good rate on tickets..."

"Sure, ok," he interrupted. "Let me see what coverage I can get. I'll talk to Allison."

Allison watched him. As he talked to Lex, he ran his hands through his hair, something he did out of habit whenever he was trying to process information he didn't quite understand. He spoke softly, his voice calm even though his face gave away his concern.

"Yeah, Mom, love you too. I'll let you know. Yes, today," he told Lex.

"She wants to go to the condo...now," he stated.

"You look worried, what's wrong with going to Hawaii?" Allison asked him.

"You know she hasn't been there since before Mom died," he replied.

"And?" Allison responded.

Aiden had been there a few times alone and with Allison on their honeymoon, but Lex never wanted to go: "It's too hard," she told him every time.

"I promised I would go whenever she was ready..." he began.

"...and you don't want to go?" Allison finished his statement.

"No, it's not that. I'm sure I can swap," he explained. "I feel like something is wrong. My mom...she is never impulsive. You know her, everything is well thought out, well-planned."

Allison cuddled up to his chest, offering her thoughts:

"It sounds like she is ready to move on a bit. Finally. That's a good thing. Maybe the impulsiveness is her way of acting on it before she changes her mind."

"Yeah?"

"What do I know, I'm just a psychiatrist," she said with a laugh. "Seriously, though, it's Hawaii. You love that place. And Avery has never been there. This could be the best way for Lex to move forward. And the best we can do is be there with her. That she wants us there is a good thing. Come on, let's be impulsive."

Logically, this made sense to Aiden. But Lex had not been the same Lex since Lilah got sick. She was Mom, sure. She was Grandma, sure. Something changed and not just the way that death changes people or changes family dynamics. She was a different person: same smile, smart, level headed, but different.

"I'm concerned, Allison," he told her. "I know that you know my mother as much as anyone could know her, but this is the Lex you've always known. She was different before."

"Are you different?" Allison asked.

"I guess I am. Yes," he responded.

"People change, Aiden," Allison offered. "You know that. What I know about your mother, that I agree with you on, is that she isn't impulsive. So, following that, she must have been thinking about this for a while. That she called you at..." Allison looked at the clock, "4 a.m.? Ugh, it's so early, anyway, that she called this early is a Lex thing: Night is night, morning is morning, she really never seems to follow time. Tell you what, if something is wrong, at least we will be there, but trying to figure her out will not help, isn't that what you told me?"

"Sure." He kissed the top of her head, giving up on trying to explain to her something he couldn't explain to himself.

Allison knew he was dismissing her; it was a classic dismissive tactic. It was his place to worry about his mother, and she knew better than to try to convince him of anything else. Lex wasn't readable. If you saw her, it was because she let you. Was she a bit dark? Perhaps. A bit depressed? Yes. More than what she put out there? Absolutely. Allison loved that in a person.

And so, six shifts changed, seven group sessions covered, one dog left with Aiden's friend, four suitcases packed and 78 hours later, the plane began its descent into Kahului.

13

The island was bathed in sunlight highlighting a mixture of lush green and red land exclusive to Hawaii. Of all the islands they had visited over the years, this was the one they called home. Maui was the right dry and calm. And contained less visible bugs, which Lilah insisted on with her "no bugs of any kind, respecting their necessity, but stay away from me" policy. Al was here, his ashes scattered a decade ago one brisk Haleakala dawn.

With everyone safe, at least temporarily, Lex could focus. And because everyone was safe, the weight of the island filled Lex's senses. The warm sweet ocean air filled her lungs, the waves sparkled as sunlight beamed through large random clouds. To the north, rain bathed the hillside.

"That guy is flying!" Avery called out excitedly.

"Yes, he is," Aiden told her. "It's called parasailing. When you are five, you can try it if you would like to."

Avery's face was pressed to the window in awe.

"What if I fall?" she asked.

Aiden chuckled.

"You won't fall, that big parachute will hold you up," he shot Allison a grin, "besides, Mommy will go with you."

Allison hit his arm before he finished offering her up. She hadn't appreciated the experience as much as he had.

Lex sighed deeply.

'Baby, you'll find, there's only one love yours and mine...'
-Lionel Richie

Lilah's song, her favorite, filled Lex's head and threatened her composure. Exactly why she didn't want to be here: Lilah driving a rented convertible, the sun intensifying the sweet smell of a road still wet from a quick tropical shower, Lex's bare feet on the dash, the taste of fresh pineapple on her lips, Aiden strapped in the back seat giggling wildly at the wind in his face, "Faster, Mommy, go faster!"

'...you are the sun, you are the rain that makes my life this foolish game'

She fought to push it away.

Allison could sense her trepidation: Lex was holding her cellphone so tightly that her fingertips were white, and Allison wondered if they were moving too quickly.

"Stop at Safeway on the way in?" she asked her.

"Sure...might as well get that out of the way," Lex replied absently.

They drove in silence with the windows down, taking in the sounds unique to the island, and she watched Avery straining to get as close to the window as the booster seat allowed, her eyes wide with anticipation and discovery. Lex felt a small pang of jealousy for the child's excitement and longed for a simpler time when all of this was new and unexplored for her as well.

"Drop us at Front Street. By Ululani," she told Aiden, realizing that this sounded like more of an order than a request, and she made a mental note to soften her tone.

She leaned back on the headrest and closed her eyes for the rest of the journey.

"Front Street," Aiden called out thoughtfully as he pulled over.

"Thank you, son," she told him as he released Avery from her seat, "Will you pick up some pineapple and bottled water? And goldfish crackers. Maybe some POG for Avery since it will be new to her."

"And candy," Avery added as she reached out for Lex's hand.

"No. We are going to get something better," she told the child.

Even with the pressure at home, the emotional roller coaster she was on, Lex couldn't imagine passing up Hawaiian Ice from their favorite place.

"Gramma, what one should I pick?" Avery asked, looking at the flavor board.

"Well, what is your favorite flavor?" Lex asked.

"Blue," Avery answered.

Lex laughed.

"Yes, I know blue, but what does blue taste like?" she asked her.

"I don't know, it tastes like blue," Avery answered.

Lex ordered:

"I'll have a *Lahaina*, large, she'll have blue, small. Do one half blue raspberry and one half in whatever other color blue you have. No snowcap."

"I like it," Avery offered, her mouth now blue, "it tastes like two kinds of blue."

She reached over and put her spoon in Lex's.

"Hey, that's banana," she observed.

"You're right," Lex told her, "tomorrow, maybe you can try red."

Hesitantly, Lex snapped a picture of Avery with her treat, thinking of Lilah and the file of Hawaiian Ice shots, taken for almost every one they ever ate. She imagined that Aiden would like the picture, and it was probably a good tradition for them. She hoped that he would continue to come here no matter what happened.

Lilah always tried different flavor combinations and always returned to her favorite: red raspberry, mango and pineapple with a snowcap. Lex pictured Lilah sitting across from her; she would be shivering, having eaten all of that soft ice and sugar quickly, and her lips would be super red or blue or whatever color was dominant.

"I'm sooo cold!!" she pictured Lilah exclaiming with a smile, pulling a silk wrap over her arms.

"Babe, slow down," Lex would have probably said with a laugh, having eaten hers just as fast.

"Mom, you ready?"

Aiden's voice caused her to turn quickly, and when she looked back, Lilah was gone...

14

The condo was on the tenth floor of a resort along the Kaanapali shore with a balcony that looked directly at the ocean and north to Black Rock. It was two bedrooms, two bathrooms with a den that Lex had arranged to have converted into a bedroom for Avery after Aiden and Allison's honeymoon. She'd called ahead, having housekeeping come in to clean and open the windows in anticipation of their arrival, and her management company once again asked if she wanted to sell, because she rarely used the place and she never rented it out, which was the main reason to have a management company. She told them no as she always did, knowing that she personally had no intention to ever return, but that Aiden would, and really, this was going to be his one day.

Walking into the living room: furniture, photos, decor... all a snapshot of time four years past, caused Lex to silently catch her breath. On the balcony, Lex took in a deep breath of the fresh salty air and held it as she closed her eyes. The soft sound of waves and voices from below mixed with Avery's vocal delight over her new bedroom intermingled with Allison's and Aiden's light conversation. As she exhaled, there was a brief moment of calm where Lex could almost pretend that Lilah was there.

She heard herself let out a long sigh and paused briefly to collect herself before making her way through the condo to their bedroom. The room was as they had left it: a collection of Lex's lip balms and perfumes still on the bedside table, a collection of travel and activity magazines and lotions on Lilah's. A single fresh white rose sat on Lex's pillow, and it startled her at first, but reading the card and catching a lump in her throat, it was pure Lilah...

"...I knew you'd come back. Don't forget pictures. I love you, Lexi..."

"Henry," Lex said out loud. No wonder he sounded relieved when she told him they would be coming. The thought haunted her: Lilah conspiring with him, meaning Lilah picturing Lex's future alone, life moving on without her...

'I'm here without you, baby, but you're still with me in my dreams...' -Three Doors Down

She sat on the bed, rubbed some of Lilah's lotion on her hands and laid back against the headboard for a few moments taking in the scent that was uniquely Lilah. Then, shaking off the sadness, Lex pulled out her computer and swallowed an Ativan that, as tiny as it was, felt hard to swallow. She logged into her security system to check the settings, ensuring a notification would ping her if anyone approached the perimeter of her house. So far, it had been quiet: mailman at 1:40 p.m., Mrs. Harrison walking Jester. Quiet.

Lex tapped into traffic security cameras around the Econolodge.

"Stupid city," she muttered, frustrated that her only shot of the area was the street just past the driveway and near a 7-11 a few blocks away. Of course, the Econolodge didn't have any accessible cameras on the property. She would have to risk paying someone to put something together. Or she would have to do it herself.

Aiden knocked quietly on her door.

"Can I come in?" he asked cautiously, opening the door and stepping in before she answered.

"Of course," she answered, faking a smile.

"Everything good?" he asked her.

Lex nodded.

He continued, "We're going to take Avery to look around and let her play in the pool before it gets dark and then get dinner. Did you want to come with us?"

"No. Have a good time. I set up snorkeling for tomorrow. I figured it would be nice to get out on a catamaran," she told him.

"Sounds great," Aiden responded, leaving her to whatever she was doing on the computer.

"Aiden?" she called after him as he walked out, "I love you, you know that, right?"

"Sure, Mom, love you too."

"How is she?" Allison asked when they had settled by the pool.

"I don't know," he answered honestly, "better than I thought, maybe. She's on autopilot."

"Could be worse," she commented.

"True. I guess we just enjoy the time with her and hope she will tell us if she needs..." Aiden stopped talking abruptly, reminding himself that his mother never really needed anything, and then continued, "well I guess we just enjoy the time."

They stayed vigilant.

The days seemed to pass quickly, and Lex couldn't say for sure that she was happy. Or sad. She just 'was.' Every activity was a reality that Lex might be looking at her family enjoying themselves for the last time. Every activity reminded her that Lilah was gone. And this being Lilah's favorite place made that reality worse. These new memories without her seemed selfish, and yet standing on the balcony watching Allison play with Avery on the shore and watching Aiden surf, well, attempt to surf, was just as if she was watching herself play with Aiden while watching Lilah surf, again, attempt to, and it gave her a bittersweet calm that nothing else could.

On her phone, Lex watched the car parked by her house on security footage. She guessed Jacob Staley was trying to figure out where they were. Should she confront him? Too risky. If she turned him in, he would still exist. He would be there for a possible someday. He had been stalking them, he was on the run. What did he want?

It mattered and yet didn't matter: Lex was calm now, focused and ready to handle him. Ready to make sure that he never interacted with her family. Whatever that meant, she didn't completely know. What mattered was that she would take care of it. But that was for tomorrow, after they returned to Los Angeles. In this moment, what mattered was in front of her: Her family laughing together, beautiful in the setting Hawaiian sun.

15

"I'm glad to hear from you," LilyQ said. She was fully formed now, the avatar, clothed casually, and the voice that at first had been robotic was now becoming more female.

"The nightmares are killing me," Lex typed.

She had been home for two days and had barely slept.

"Tell me about them," LilyQ said.

"Everyone is dead. I'm dead," she said out loud.

"Did someone die recently?" the voice asked.

Lex contemplated her response. Where would she even begin? A lot of people died.

"Recently, no," she replied cautiously.

"Are you afraid of dying?" LilyQ asked.

"Of dying, yes. Of death, no. I have a lot going on right now," Lex replied cautiously.

"Tell me," typed in the text balloon.

"I don't think I can share this with you," Lex said honestly.

"Fair enough," LilyQ stated, "but we should start somewhere. Tell me about the first time someone in your life died."

"Too personal," Lex typed.

There was a pause in the response, and Lex wondered if LilyQ was struggling to figure out what to say.

"If this is going to work for you, you are going to have to do the work, and that means sharing. Trust me, I think we can agree that we have a unique bond now," she said finally.

Lex thought about the woman and those two small children. What were they doing? Did they feel safe? It was hard not to ask if she knew anything. She sighed. Not knowing protected her. Still, it was quite an intricate task, and it was hard not to see the results. She chose her words carefully:

"I sent you a link for next time," Lex offered.

"You assume," said the avatar.

"I know," Lex answered confidently.

"Got it. I'll let you know," was the response.

Lex knew why she was having nightmares. She had them all her life before Lilah. And then, with Lilah, they happened only occasionally until Lilah got sick. No Lilah, no peace. And now Jacob Staley, what was she going to do?

"Let's make a deal. I'll share something about myself with you, and then you can decide if you want to share with me," the computer therapist offered.

"I thought that therapists were supposed to be neutral blank slates," Lex replied.

"I think the ethical ship has sailed."

The response made Lex laugh. "True that," she said.

LilyQ began telling her a story:

"So, then. Death. Let me tell you about my reality..."

LilyQ's cousin, a toddler, died in the December LilyQ turned 20, right after her birthday and right before Christmas. The last time she saw him before that, they had come to visit and she remembered that she was curling her hair in the other room, listening to her aunt talk to her grandmother about her husband.

"...I would have left if he had ever laid a hand on me," her grandmother told her, referring to her grandfather.

At the time, she was nineteen and already completely numb to the past so the comment had neither surprised nor angered her. She could see it in her cousin's eyes, his beautiful dark soulless eyes: at two years old, he already knew what life was. She should have screamed at them, told her, "What the fuck?! Get out of there, you guys don't deserve this!" She instead said nothing. She didn't even leave the bathroom.

She and her best friend at the time shared the December birthday one day apart, and they celebrated that particular December weekend with their friends: drugs and alcohol, right on target for what she called her next weight loss attempt. Up all night and then a quick nap before church, LilyQ thought they must have looked like death that Sunday morning.

She could still clearly see herself pace around with a toothbrush hanging out of her mouth, the leftover Everclear taste now thoroughly mixed with mint as she flipped through a coloring book that she and a friend had spent most of the night coloring, creatively channeling both Dali and Basquiat. They had skillfully colored the whole book, all while watching movies, though she only remembered actually watching *E.T.*

Her friend had a family obligation to go to church that Sunday morning, so they went. She had tried rather unsuccessfully to appear normal and was sure it was funny. Funny and very disrespectful.

"I mean, who goes to church wasted?" LilyQ mused, interrupting her own narration.

She was sure it was right up there with the time she and her cousin went with a friend to church, and they were taking communion and her cousin went up to the altar and came back to the pew, opened her hand and said, "What am I supposed to do with this?" In her hand was the communion wafer, and LilyQ and her friend started laughing and her mom looked over in frustration that they were laughing and probably because her cousin had no idea what she was doing.

If her friend's parents suspected something, they were very polite and didn't mention it. LilyQ figured that they must have known she and her friend were completely hung over because they insisted on them eating breakfast. LilyQ remembered that everything smelled both perfect and nauseating at the same time and that she was so nauseous at the thought of food that she could taste the empty stomach bile watering in her mouth. Eating defeated the whole purpose of using amphetamines in the first place, so she nibbled at food and pushed it around her plate.

She explained the look of death away by saying they were up all night and just extremely tired, which was completely true. All they cared about was making it through breakfast so that they could both try to take a nap before work. Once her head hit the pillow, of course, she couldn't sleep because she was still really high, and LilyQ laid there staring at the ceiling, not knowing for how long. Finally, a phone ringing faintly down the hall broke the silence, and she listened to her friend's mother talking. LilyQ heard her come down the hall, stopping in the doorway:

"It's your grandmother." The woman looked worried as she handed LilyQ the phone.

"Hello?" she said, wondering how her grandmother even was able to locate her.

"Your uncle killed himself and Michael. They're dead. You need to come home."

"What?" She remembered saying that clearly and remembered feeling her eyes getting hot.

"Your aunt and cousin don't know yet, they are driving back right now from the airport with your uncle's mother and sister. The police called us to meet them there."

"Ok, I'll be there," she told her on autopilot.

Her friend's mom hugged her, was she crying? She couldn't remember, but her friend looked at her apologetically because of the hug. LilyQ didn't mind, she could barely stop shaking from the shock.

As her friend was driving her home, she passed by a mental health facility and remembered saying something like, "Maybe you should just drop me off there." She definitely remembered laughing coldly, saying something like:

"It never ends...my family is so fucked!" and all she could think was 'How is my cousin going to be now?' The world was already so dark, and she admitted that she was already pretty hateful.

"I hate to admit it, but I felt relieved that this violent death had not come to take my other cousin because, as bad as it was, I knew her longer, and it would have been harder, I think," she said.

LilyQ felt guilty, though, knowing that her cousin would be living a nightmare that never ends. Because for her, even after loss, after a nightmare realized, LilyQ still had nightmares...

Lex could relate. Nightmares were all she had, so much so that they were as much a part of her memories as any real event:

The clown. Her sister tied to a table and Lexi tied to a chair while her sister was tortured and killed slowly by the clown, and all she could do was scream and watch, and when it was all over, Lexi realized that she wasn't tied to the chair at all...

"...and anyway, the drive to the police station was blurred," LilyQ continued.

LilyQ was outside of herself in the car listening but not connected to her grandmother's words: that her aunt, uncle and cousins were staying in a hotel overnight to pick up his mother and sister from the airport for Christmas; that there was a fight, and he threw her aunt against the wall and left with Michael, leaving her cousin to take care of her mom; that her aunt went to the hospital with broken ribs while her uncle went to a hardware store, bought some duct tape and a hose.

The next morning, a couple were out jogging and saw the green VW van along the side of the road. They pulled open the side door and there was her uncle and Michael, and just to really say fuck you, her cousin's dog, all dead, and the police left a note on her aunt's door for her to come to the police station and somehow got in touch with her grandmother. Their hope was that they got there before she did so that at least someone close to them could break the news. LilyQ remembered thinking that was ironic: closeness wasn't really a family thing.

Two grief counselors were already lined up and took them to a room to help prepare her grandmother to tell her aunt this horrible, unimaginable news. But how do you prepare someone to tell her daughter that her husband has murdered her baby?

"I think I paced around for ten eternities, listening to the hum of their voices and then finally I paused and said, 'You are not going to tell them together are you? You can't make my cousin be there for that. It isn't fair," LilyQ said.

Even in her semi-drugged up head, LilyQ knew that her cousin needed to stay the child, with her own child grief, and her aunt, the mom. Especially with this. She thought it would be worse for her cousin to have to see her mother's reaction to that news. That was a private hell, and they had at least agreed.

So, they waited. LilyQ kept looking at the clock but could never remember what time it was the last time she looked. A counselor was talking to her, and she was responding, though she admitted that she couldn't hear what the counselor was saying or what she herself was saying; there had been a deafening white noise in her ears that she kept trying to shake off.

And then they arrived, and LilyQ felt her heart stop and then beat out of her chest. Her grandmother stayed in the back, and she went with one of the counselors to the front. As soon as LilyQ saw them, her head cleared, and they quickly took her cousin aside. She remembered her aunt's eyes: they were questioning, confused. LilyQ looked away.

The counselors escorted her cousin into a small, dimly lit room. She held her cousin's hand. As the counselor began to tell her, LilyQ heard a soul-crushing scream of anguish from down the hall.

"...truly, there is no other way to describe it other than soul-crushing. I have never heard that sound since. It haunts me still," she said.

Her cousin asked about her dog. The counselor shook her head, and it was then that her cousin cried. All they could do was hold her; there were no words that could properly fill the room. There was only the deafening weight of anguish.

After, her cousin and aunt spent a few minutes together, her aunt was blank and broken. LilyQ drove her cousin to her house. It was a sobering drive.

"I bet you are really tired," LilyQ told her. "You can lay here and go to sleep if you want to."

Her cousin laid across the front seat of her truck, resting her head on LilyQ's leg as she drove. LilyQ ran her fingers through her hair as she drove. Her cousin slept quickly and deeply.

'So, what now?' she thought.

She felt pretty awful to admit it, but she finally felt relieved. Her cousin was with her, and she was safe. Whatever went on was no more, and that gave her enough comfort to breathe.

Later, when everyone was all together, the discomfort was too much to bear, and LilyQ escaped to her place of work to talk to her friend and tell her what happened. Her friend was working their shift alone, and she thanked her for covering. It had felt so good to get away from the uncomfortable anguish for a few minutes.

Her aunt and cousin stayed with them for a couple days while the rest of the family found their way out to them from other parts of the country, and LilyQ stayed away most of that time, grateful to have a full work schedule.

One of the days, they went to her aunt's house, and her aunt walked mechanically past Michael's room, shutting the door without looking. Her uncle's sister and mom were there. How horrible for them this must have been. She remembered his mother saying that she just couldn't believe it. The sister looked so lost. LilyQ hugged her. She didn't even know the woman's name. She held on for a while.

"I'm sorry this happened," she told the sister quietly and LilyQ admitted to Lex that honestly, even now, she still doesn't really know why she said it. That day, they removed the Christmas presents and the tree. What was there to celebrate? As the tree was hauled out, something hit the floor: a small piece of candy wrapped in Christmas paper with a tag: *'To Daddy, Love Michael'* written in her cousin's handwriting. LilyQ went outside and cried silently alone.

Another day before the funeral, LilyQ went with some family members to retrieve personal items from the van at the impound lot. She remembered staring out into the desert on the seemingly endless drive. In a daze, she pulled duct tape off the back window of the van. As she removed each piece, she pictured it being put on. She imagined Michael sitting on the floor of the van, playing with a toy, and the dog wagging his tail, happy and clueless. She pictured their last moments and was thankful that he was too young to know he was being murdered by the person who should have been his hero.

Before throwing away the grey tape, she pulled off a small piece and shoved it into her pocket. Later, she would study it slowly, morbidly trying to feel close to that moment when Michael's life slipped away. She kept the tape for days until it was too hard to think about.

LilyQ had never been to a funeral, never seen a dead body in person. She had never been in a funeral home, and she admitted it scared her a bit as she walked up to the small casket slowly, curious.

There he was, this cherub boy, who in death appeared to be peacefully sleeping: his beautiful long dark blond lashes, his blond curls brushed across his forehead. He was wearing overalls. He had a little hand-made toy in his hand.

And it was real, and it wasn't real. She couldn't feel anything and watched it like a movie. Standing over him, it was as if no one else was in the room. There was no time, no space, no air. Just his small body laid out in front of her. She touched his hand, so cool and unnatural. She touched his face and ran her fingers across the blond ringlet bangs.

"I'm sorry," she whispered to him, "I'm so fucking sorry that this was your life."

In her head, she was begging, screaming to be taken instead. How cruel and twisted was fate that she spent his last day alive wasted, not caring about anything.

She looked at him for the last time, burning his image into her brain.

The funeral director came in to take him out of the casket so that her aunt could hold him one last time. LilyQ walked out, feeling angry that everyone was here in such a private moment of hell. This wasn't theirs; they didn't belong there. She went to the car to wait for the funeral procession, and in that line of slow-moving cars, some metal song about a cemetery blared ironically from the stereo, drowning out her life.

She admitted to Lex that even now, with all of the time, all of the psychiatric training and mentoring, she still couldn't remember the service except that it was across from a grade school and she had wondered if the school was her cousin's. She could only recall how unusually cold it was and wondering how they were going to leave him there alone in a cold, dark box?

"It isn't that scary," LilyQ sometimes still heard in her head when she thought about it. It is her grandma's voice, what she would say to her when she would freak out while watching some horror movie on television.

"So, this dead oppressive silence opened up and swallowed another one of us and after, like everything that ever happened in my family, nobody talked about it," LilyQ said, and then added:

"Silence can be so...dangerous."

LilyQ stopped talking, and for a few moments, there was just a heavy awkward silence in the air.

Lex wasn't startled by the story; the details didn't faze her: The vulnerability did. It wasn't hers; it was this unknown person for unknown reasons sharing something that was or was not true. It made her uncomfortable.

"Why did you tell me this?" she asked finally.

"I thought I'd take a chance," LilyQ answered, "I think you could use someone, or somewhere, in this case, for you to be you. The real you. Secrets are a death sentence. I know that is a bit ironic considering...this. I want you to know that you can trust me, that I understand and there is nothing you can tell me that will shock me or make me stop talking to you. I want you to know that what I do is important to me on a personal level, all of what I do."

Lex had been through this before, heard the speech before: There were some things that no one could really understand or relate to.

"But you also want someone who can do what I do," Lex stated.

"Yes," LilyQ responded truthfully, "as I said, all of what I do is important. Just because this benefits me, the network, doesn't mean that you cannot benefit...beyond easy access to medication, right? I'm good at what I do."

"In my experience...I don't really find it helpful to talk about who I've seen dead, or what I have done." Lex hesitated before continuing, "But I did something, and it's come back around."

"Are you in danger?" LilyQ inquired.

She responded carefully, "That is a good question. I don't know yet, but really...I just need to deal with it before it gets away from me."

"What can I do to help you?" typed across the text box.

"Nothing. Seriously, I shouldn't have even said that much," Lex stated solemnly.

"You haven't said anything," LilyQ observed.

"What I said is enough. It's my problem. I have loose ends to tie," Lex said truthfully.

"What can I do to help?" the Avatar asked.

"I guess I don't know. I don't think there is anything," Lex said, adding, "don't let this stop you from using the link, though. I need to keep busy, and really, I'm at my best if I'm multitasking, so I'd take advantage of that right now, whoever you are."

"You sure?" LilyQ typed.

"Yes. Whatever this is...I don't care, take advantage while you can," Lex advised.

That might have been understated, considering her issue.

"And you will let me know if there is anything I can do?" LilyQ asked.

"This is mine to do," she responded.

"Be safe," popped up in the text balloon.

"Thanks," Lex typed back.

Lex closed the link. What was the constant in her head? Killing Melissa was easy, because Melissa didn't see it coming. Her brother, though? He was a big guy, and violent. Plus, he had enough sense to get a different identity. She guessed he wasn't smart enough or educated enough to create his own. Someone somewhere was hopefully smart enough to stay in the shadows. Was there an active search for him? It had been several weeks. So, why wait? What was he up to? What did he want? He couldn't know that she was responsible for his sister's death. Could he?

'Don't be paranoid,' she thought.

It was a gift that he didn't know that Lex knew who he was or where he was staying. It was her turn to do some stalking.

She spent the next few hours going over this in her head: all the details, all the things that could go wrong and how to compensate for surprises.

"Lex?" she heard from the front door.

"In here," she called back, switching the television to the news.

"Everything ok?" Allison asked her.

"Absolutely, why do you ask?" she responded.

"Hi, Gramma," Avery said to her as she took off down the hallway to her room.

"You never double lock the door," Allison observed.

"Oh," Lex thought quickly. "Some burglaries in the area. I'm sure it's fine, it just felt safer."

Allison, already running behind, turned to leave. Her backpack brushed against a shelf, knocking a snow globe onto the floor. It was a cheap plastic souvenir, the kind that is always blue and white. This one had a Hollywood sign in it.

"Oh, damn, sorry," she said as she picked it up and turned it over and around, adding "not broken."

"I'm not worried about it," Lex stated.

Allison shook it and watched the 'snow' swirl and fall.

"Hollywood must have been a crazy place to live," she said.

"A lifetime ago. Lilah got that for me as a joke. I hate those things," Lex offered.

Allison placed it back on the shelf, saying, "Aiden told me that you have quite the stories from that time."

"True," Lex said easily, "too many."

"Did you live there a long time?" Allison asked.

"A couple years..."

"Did you like it? Was it fun?"

'I do not have time for this,' Lex thought, but she couldn't just rush Allison out the door. Allison was too smart for that. She would know something was up. Lex searched her Hollywood past for something to quell the young woman's curiosity.

"Well, sure, when I first moved there, it was exciting and weird and crazy, so I loved it. I mean, my first day as I was headed to the Vine Lodge Hotel, where I ended up living for about a month, someone was throwing belongings out of a second story window, screaming something

incoherent. I thought it was awesome. I was young...and also careless and overconfident," Lex shared honestly. "I did enjoy walking Hollywood boulevard at night. It was always quiet and easy to think about everything and nothing. Eventually, it just stopped being interesting."

"Is that why you left, because it stopped being interesting?" Allison asked.

Living in Hollywood had finally lost its appeal at a gas station one Saturday on her way to get her nails done. Lex had been lost in thought, imagining Lilah still curled up sleeping in her bed where Lex had just left her when voice startled her:

"I can pump that for you," a teenage boy stated. He seemed to have come from nowhere.

"No, I've got it," she replied.

"Please. I just need a ride to Gower," he pleaded sweetly.

Lex sized him up. The boy was well built, almost too skinny. He had straight black hair and light brown pants. She decided that though he looked strong, he appeared harmless, so she figured why not?

She handed him the nozzle.

They left the gas station and took a shortcut through a residential neighborhood, Lex not really paying attention to him.

"You like what you see?" he asked her.

Lex looked over at the young man, and he had unzipped his pants and pulled his penis out. He was smiling and holding it with both hands like a prize.

She pulled over quickly and stared him in the eyes.

"You like what you see?" he said again.

Lex smiled and said calmly," Are you fucking high?"

His smile faded.

"Zip up your fucking pants," she demanded.

He started to reach for the car handle.

"Oh, no way," she told him and took off, laughing as she drove.

"Seriously, I could be some psycho. Then what?" she asked him.

He was quiet.

"Look, I'll drop you off at Gower, just like you asked, but Jesus...either you are a dumbass, or a pervert and what goes around comes around. So, which is it?"

Lex was driving pretty fast now, and his look told her she must have sounded like the psycho she told him she could be.

"I'm not a pervert," he stated quietly.

"Ah."

"I'm not," he insisted.

"Well, I'm not interested either way, dumbass."

They approached the salon on Gower and Lex began to slow the car.

"A little advice," she offered him. "I'd work on your people reading skills. If this is how you are surviving, you better wise up, or you will end up dead. Being a guy doesn't make you invincible. A lot of us are pretty nuts."

She stopped the car.

"Better still, find something else," she told him.

He got out of the car and walked away quickly. Lex watched him, laughing at his shocked expression.

Remembering this, Lex wondered if she really did scare him. She'd lost too many 'friends' to the night that was Hollywood.

"I grew up," Lex replied to Allison's question finally, "The last straw...I got pulled over by the police because they were looking to bust people for drugs. Coincidently, at that exact time, I was exiting a Burger King parking lot, a random homeless person put his hands through my window on the passenger side asking for money. I guess the police thought I was buying drugs. So, I was standing there while they searched my food...which by the way, they were very careful not to actually touch, so that I could eat it, while another officer patted me down and asked me to take my hair out of a bun to check for drugs. I thought to myself, *'Yeah, I'm over this,'* And, well, Lilah didn't like it. So, I moved."

"Hmm," Allison said, "And you weren't afraid, living there by yourself?"

"No, it wasn't that big of a deal," she answered, shrugging.

Allison looked down at her watch. "Oh, damn, I'm late... you have to tell me more later, ok?"

"Sure," Lex answered, glad that the information she shared had distracted Allison enough to make her forget the locked door.

She put Jacob and her plans away...a short reprieve. He would have to wait...she was with Avery now.

16

Late that same evening, Lex watched the dark chaos of the busy street from her vehicle. It was intimidating, stepping out from behind the safety of the computer, but there she was, sitting in her SUV five blocks from the EconoLodge. In this location, she could easily see vehicles come and go, and Lex waited in the dark silence for him to leave. Lilah's voice filled her head telling her to go to the police, that there was still time to turn him in, get him out of their lives and allow her time to find a better way to get rid of him.

If she hadn't killed his sister maybe.

'Don't do it, Lex.'

This had been her routine for several nights. The first night, he left at 10 p.m., and she followed him for just a few blocks, then, worried he might see her, she'd turned and went home. The next night, she sat waiting, and he left a bit later. That night, she waited for him to return, which he did around 2 a.m. For the next two nights, she watched. He had a routine: The time was off maybe half an hour, but it was the same routine. On the fifth night, she followed him once again, careful to stay back far enough to lose him, which she almost did a couple times.

Lex wasn't surprised to find his destination was a bar, nor was she surprised to see him take a woman to his car for what she assumed was extremely rough sex, considering she could hear the woman screaming from across the parking lot. They made their way back into the bar not much later.

This was a dangerous game. Jacob was watching her. Sometimes, he sat in his car down the street. Sometimes, he followed her as she ran errands. Lex was cautious, never leaving the house with Avery. Through her security cameras, she would see him pull up and sit, never for long, but sometimes more than once in a day. She purposely found places to go to ensure that he would follow. He always did, but if he was trying to find a routine, he was never going to find it. She kept an eye on the security cameras around Aiden's apartment, around the hospital, not taking for granted that he could have hurt them already, and it felt like a gift that he hadn't been impulsive. She knew that wouldn't last forever.

A week of watching him and now, sure of a routine, she waited. As expected, Jacob pulled out of the parking lot. Hesitantly, Lex pulled a tablet from her bag and with a few lines of code, a six-block radius went dark. She pulled a pair of gloves out of the console and put them on. She could feel her body temperature rise and her heartbeat increase.

Lex was scared. She didn't want to admit that to herself, but how could she ignore it? She was out of her league. Her place was in front of a computer and anonymous. Finding someone else to do this, though, meant involving someone else...meaning someone else would know. A secret was only a secret if you never told anyone. She was scared, but she was driven. No one threatened her family. Ever.

'Don't do it, Lex.'

"Lilah, I don't have a choice," she said out loud, collecting herself.

The room was easy to break into, and it certainly wasn't her first time, it had just been a long time. Cheap hotel, cheap locks. The screen was open, and Jacob didn't bother to lock the deadbolt. Lex thought he must have been really confident, or really ignorant. Though she knew she had time, she hurried through, shining a flashlight in the darkness of a room with old blackout curtains. In her haste, she hit her ankle against a bedpost and almost fell over.

"Fuck," she said out loud, too loud as an intruder, and caught her mouth with her hand.

Pictures of Melissa were taped to the wall next to the bed. One of them Lex recognized from the apartment she had shared with Aiden. One was of Melissa, and, she assumed, Jacob as young teenagers, looking more like a couple than brother and sister.

"Jesus," she whispered under her breath.

Lex shined the flashlight further down the wall and stopped on a picture of Avery in her bathing suit on her front lawn. It must have been taken the day of Aiden's party. Next to it was a modified picture, it had been one with Melissa, Aiden and Avery. She recognized it. Lilah had taken that picture when Avery was three months old. Aiden's face had been cut out, and Jacob's face was taped in. There was a picture of Lex as well, at least, Lex assumed it was, though the face had been scribbled out in red marker. Or maybe blood.

The pictures, as disturbing as they were, at least confirmed to Lex what she had concluded: Jacob Staley had come for what he thought was his. The thought made her feel physically cold, then hot, then sick in the fear of what never was: that Avery could have ended up with this man, this dangerous and obviously very angry man. Luckily, Lex had ruined that plan. Her own anger quickly replaced fear. Whatever this was, whatever his plan, she appeared to be the focus of his anger, but it was clear that he was here for Avery. Her hands ached to rip the pictures off the wall, but she moved on, telling herself that he would never get near Avery. Or her son. Or, for that matter, Allison.

The room itself was surprisingly clean and well organized except for the broken mirror above the sink. On top of the dresser were several little toy ponies all arranged as if they were in a stable. These were the kind that Avery liked.

'He's observant,' Lex thought.

She flipped through a calendar hanging next to the dresser. It was clean and out of place in the outdated room, and she noticed that October 12 was circled.

"There it is," she said out loud, disturbingly pleased with herself in spite of the dire seriousness of this situation: Jacob had a plan that had something to do with three weeks from now.

Suddenly, the thought, *'Over my dead body'* seemed more tangible. Lex realized that this was probably going to be messy. Lex hated mess. But a plan, she could work with. She left the room cautiously and thanked the heavens for the gift of borrowed time.

17

"How are you doing?" LilyQ asked.

"I'm just awesome," Lex typed.

Looking at the avatar, she mused its current form.

'I built my own personalized therapist,' she thought as LilyQ continued her questions:

"Are you sleeping?"

"Sometimes. I saw the link," Lex responded.

"What do you think?"

"I think that sometimes people suffer inwardly, and sometimes people suffer outwardly, causing chaos and pain to those around them. I think the best possible outcome would be to stop the suffering either way."

"Is this something that you are comfortable with?" LilyQ asked.

Lex took her time answering so as not to seem too eager, instead opting for a non-answer:

'When my child was very young, my neighbor hung himself, so yeah, I understand mental illness..."

"You have children?" LilyQ inquired, interrupting her.

"Grown," Lex answered quickly, uncomfortable with how easily she broke her own rule by sharing this, but it probably didn't matter anymore considering what was in front of her now.

LilyQ continued: "Are you sure you are ok?"

"Wow," Lex responded, "first you tell me to share personal information so that you can help me, and I do, and you think there is something wrong? What is it with you people?"

"I don't think there is anything wrong; it was unexpected," LilyQ responded.

"Should I continue?" she asked the therapist.

"Of course."

Lex continued while throwing the ball for the dog:

"So, this neighbor, was a teacher, retired, but he taught a class or two at a community college once in a while. He had a younger wife, and they had a baby. Their child was a bit younger than mine. This was while I worked from home, and he started coming over randomly, never really to visit, just to ask random things like if I had gotten my mail the day before or to borrow socks for his child, saying that he couldn't find any.

It was Halloween. My yard was decorated with gravestones, little skeletons in children's overalls, zombie parts scattered on the lawn, all of the good stuff. I also had a scarecrow hanging from a noose. My neighbor walked past my yard several times over that couple weeks, but I didn't think it was unusual at the time.

It was a morning a few days after Halloween, and my child was actually taking a nap, so I seized the opportunity to take a shower. When I got out, I heard someone knocking on my door. I was just in a towel, so I didn't go to the door right away, and by the time I had put on a bathrobe, no one was there. Later that day, I was outside putting away the Halloween decorations, and my child was running around the yard chasing a ball, laughing in that little kid giggle, you know, the one that they always outgrow and, as a parent, you miss when they get older.

My neighbor's wife pulled into the driveway, and we waved to each other as her garage door opened: he was hanging there with a plastic grocery bag over his head. I can't remember if I saw him before, after or at the same time she screamed out, but she jumped out of the car and ran in, reaching up and pulling the bag off his head while simultaneously trying to hold him up. Their baby was in the car seat in the back of her car."

Lex paused for a moment, then asked out of curiosity, "Considering what you are asking from me, have you ever seen anyone dead from hanging?"

"No, not at the time they were hanging," LilyQ responded.

Lex sighed before continuing, not so much about what she was sharing but at the thought of Aiden's little child laugh.

"His face was translucent, but purple as well. His lips and nose were purple, and his swollen tongue had pushed out of his mouth just a bit. It was also purple. He was very dead.

I yelled out to her something like, "Hang on, I'm coming," grabbing my child as I ran into my house, who I tossed into a chair on my way to the kitchen, saying, "Stay here," as I grabbed a knife from the drawer and yelled out for someone to call 911."

Lex paused. The person she had yelled to was Lilah, but Lex couldn't bring herself to say it. Sharing Lilah wasn't part of the deal. Especially in something like this, since it had traumatized them for quite a while, especially her Lilah, who had known him much better.

162

"I ran over and tossed her the knife, and she cut him down with one whack. He was, literally, dead weight, and his head hit the concrete hard. It sounded just like a splitting watermelon might sound if dropped on the floor.

She gave him CPR. I know she knew he was dead, but it was her husband, so she had to try, I guess. As she pumped his chest, this pink foam came out of his mouth. I took their child out of the car into my house. My child was still sitting in the chair. It's funny, but that is what I remember more than anything else, the picture clear in my head, seeing my child in the chair waiting for permission to get up.

Later...after the ambulance and police, after my neighbor's wife came and got her child and was whisked away by her family, after the funeral...I found out that he had gone to his wife's work and dropped off their child, telling her that he had an appointment. She knew something was off about that, which is why she came home early."

"What was it like for you?" LilyQ asked.

"Front row seats to someone else's horror show? It was surreal, completely unexpected. Honestly, I was relieved to have taken down the hanging scarecrow before she found her husband like that. I was in awe that while my child was outside laughing, he was hanging there dying. I was mad that he must have been aware that he would be discovered in daylight and also right around the time that kids would be walking home from school. And for a while, I felt responsible, at least partly, because I know it was him knocking on the door that morning, and I didn't answer."

"It wasn't your fault that he killed himself," LilyQ offered.

"Sure. If someone is determined to die, they will die. He was obviously determined. If I would have answered the door, more than likely, the only difference would have been that he would have asked me to watch his son while he did it. But I still wonder...if I had gotten to the door before he walked away, what if something I said might have changed his mind? It is what it is, though. At least he didn't kill anyone else."

"Are you sure you are going to be ok doing this?" LilyQ asked.

"I get it," Lex replied, "I mean, I'm just facilitating. That's much different than the decision to do it, or actually doing it. The question is, this vigilante stuff, judging, are you ok doing it?"

"I am. This is what we do," LilyQ responded adamantly.

Lex closed the session.

The link contained the file of a man who, on several occasions, stopped taking his prescribed antipsychotic medication, each time attacking someone: his mother, an attendant at his living facility and lastly, two teenagers on a bus. Each time, he was hospitalized, put back on medication, then sent home. This last time, one of the teenagers was stabbed in the face. She would require several surgeries to be able to talk correctly.

Lex sent the request to a problem solver, one who specialized in taking homicide out of death's equation. He (or she) was rumored to be extremely efficient. How this person was able to do this fascinated Lex, and it scared her, but knowing exactly what the outcome would be and her role in it felt no different than playing a game of strategy: There was a problem. The problem needed to be solved. Solve the problem.

That was the plan for Jacob Staley as well.

She threw the tennis ball down the hallway, and the dog ran after it. As she continued to play with him, she thought about what to do next: She had to get the pictures from the hotel, and Jacob Staley needed to die. Or Eric Matthews needed to die. Soon.

18

As the days passed over the next week, time with Avery became precious and bittersweet, a handful of fine sand that was slowly slipping through her fingers. If Lex survived...

'If.'

...there was a good chance that in spite of her best efforts to be careful and erase any involvement, she would be caught.   Regardless, someone would need to be erased...Eric, Jacob. Or both.

Or not caught, and one of them needed to be erased. Or perhaps both of them. But that would be up to fate.

If everything backfired, if she was killed, it was set that Jacob would 'reappear' along with the paper trail of Eric Matthews as an alias. Everyone would know that he was Melissa's brother. That he was a criminal who tried to hide who he was. That he had been here for months; in other words, her death would be premeditated, and she doubted that anyone would believe anything he tried to tell them.

If she succeeded, then Jacob needed to be erased forever and Eric Matthews, a nowhere man, a mystery, would exist...well, cease to exist, as a drifter, a missing link to random burglaries, etc.

All of this intricate detail had to be considered. Records, DNA and fingerprints in databases needed to be updated or changed. The timing to release these changes needed to be set. Two different scenarios, two different paths. Risky? Yes. Doable? Yes. Was she scared that everything could go wrong? Yes.

Drawing pictures at the kitchen table with Avery that afternoon, listening to her chattering on about her dolls, she thought about Lilah and felt what she must have felt, knowing that soon she might never see her again, but for Lilah so much worse because her death had been definite. Still, the sadness of the thought of not seeing Avery grow up was overwhelming. Lilah's obsession with pictures made sense now; through them, she existed to her granddaughter in a way that just talking about her didn't capture.

But Lex could walk away. But she couldn't. Jacob Stayley could walk away. But really, he couldn't either. What was it that made them so different? Perhaps nothing. She understood him completely. Like her, he had a problem, and he needed to solve it. Was it revenge? Partly. Mostly, though, Lex understood that she and this sick, twisted, violent psycho were alike in many ways: they both wanted what was theirs, and they were willing to take or keep it in any way necessary. Maybe neither of them deserved what they desired. Maybe the best thing was that both of them were destroyed.

"Hey, Sweet Girl, do you want to see something special?" Lex asked.

"Ok," Avery replied, not looking up from her coloring.

Lex brought a small wooden jewelry box to the table and placed it in front of her.

"When you grow up, I am giving this to you," she told her.

Avery tried to open the box unsuccessfully, then picked it up and started turning it around and shaking it.

"Gramma, it's broken, it doesn't open," she stated.

Lex smiled and gently stopped her from shaking it.

"It's a magic box," she told her, "Grandma Lilah gave it to me."

"What's in it!" the child asked, shaking it again.

"All of my special treasures," Lex responded.

"Can I see them?" Avery asked her.

"Well, let's see if we can open it, shall we?" Lex replied, motioning for the child to put the box on the table.

"Hmm," Lex pondered out loud, "how to open a magic box…"

"Is there a key?" Avery asked.

Lex shook her head no.

"Are there magic words?" Avery continued her inquiry.

"Nope," Lex teased.

"Gramma! How do we open it!"

"Ok, I'm going to tell you, but it's a secret only for you."

Lex took Avery's hands in hers and placed her fingers methodically on the box:

"Pay attention now," she told the child, "Left, left, right, left."

The box clicked open.

"Go ahead," she motioned to Avery to look inside.

"Ooh, Gramma, pretty!" Avery exclaimed, pulling out pieces of jewelry: Rings, bracelets…jeweled and shiny.

"Those are mine, and some are Grandma Lilah's," Lex told her.

While Avery tried on every piece of jewelry, Lex pulled back the velvet lining in the box. Underneath was a small SD card: Every hidden bank account, amounts, passwords, instructions on how to retrieve it all without being traced. This was the real treasure, but something Avery wouldn't comprehend or need until she was much older. The instructions left were to give her the box on her 18th birthday. Lex placed the card back and replaced the velvet, closing the box.

"Ok. Let's have you try it," she said and motioned to Avery to pick up the box.

Lex worked with her over and over, repeating the words; a mantra that she hoped would trigger many years from now when the box was given to her...left, left, right, left, over and over. When Avery grew bored of this game, Lex put the box back on a shelf in her bedroom, putting her fingers to her lips then touching the box before she left it there.

She repeated this process with the child over the next few days, knowing that soon enough, everything might change.

On that Friday afternoon, Lex watched the security video focused on the street. She moved the focus down the block. Jacob was sitting in his car, eating, she guessed. He was getting bolder, more confident, she thought, as he began parking closer to the house. She checked her clock: 5 p.m. Lex was already late to take Avery home, but she couldn't risk leaving with her. She picked up the phone:

"I'd like to report a couple of young men across from my house. They look like they are doing drugs. Is it possible that you could send a patrol car around to maybe talk to them? I have a small child here, and I'd feel much safer..."

Jacob sat sweating in his car. It was ridiculously warm for a late autumn afternoon. He was hot and irritated. And over it. The small room he had been living in all these weeks was getting to him: a small hot box that only reminded him of Melissa every day. He hated Los Angeles more and more, and the women...so full of themselves, so seemingly independent...and yet they let themselves be taken so easily, let him do whatever he wanted, bordering on the edge of criminal. He preferred younger, more dependent. He needed to go somewhere that he could find someone who he could control, if the girl he was working didn't pan out. If he stayed much longer, though, he was going to really hurt someone and ruin what he'd come to do.

There was no way he was going to be able to wait any longer. Why he thought it was so important to do this on his mother's birthday was lost on him now in the sweltering heat. No. He was done. Time to get what he came for and get out.

A patrol car brought his thoughts back to the moment. It moved slowly, the officer looking side to side. He watched it pass him and round the corner slowly. Jacob casually drove away. The next time she and the kid went anywhere together. That would be the time...

19

"Traffic?" Aiden said, picking Avery up into a hug.

"Crazy," Lex replied, following him in.

"Do you want to stay for dinner?" he asked.

"Sure," Lex told him as they joined Allison in the kitchen, "what are we having?"

"I ordered a couple pizzas to pick up," he told her.

"Oh, formal dinner then," Lex said.

"Ha. Ha," he shot back.

"If you'll excuse me," Allison said, walking past them. She looked pale and upset.

"What happened?" Lex inquired.

Aiden put Avery down, telling her:

"Why don't you go put your stuff away, ok, princess?"

"Ok, Daddy," the little girl replied, running off down the hallway to her room.

He waited until she left, then quietly told Lex:

"One of the outpatients she was treating hung himself in his halfway house last night..."

Lex stopped hearing him as cold ran through her body.

'What the fuck...' she was thinking as she said, her voice calm, controlled:

"Tell you what. Why don't you take Avery with you to get food, and I'll stay and talk to her."

"I don't think she wants to talk about it, Mom," he told her, knowing why she was sending them away. "I think she really needs some space."

"Nonsense," she told him, "I'll talk to her. And when you get back, we can talk about preschool. I found a good one."

"Of course you did," he said as he motioned Avery towards the door.

"You expect any different from me?" she asked, smiling at him.

He shook his head and answered:

"Nope, not at all."

As they left, Lex steadied herself against the kitchen island. She took a deep breath that felt like swallowing her own heart as her mind raced to convince herself that this was a weird coincidence, that Allison's patient happened to hang himself and that she just set this exact scenario in motion could not be one in the same situation. This was way too close to home. She cursed LilyQ. Did she know her? Know Allison? What the fuck? Lex kicked the side of the counter before heading down the hall. When she saw Los Angeles, why didn't she think 'too close to home?' She was getting too comfortable and complacent, breaking all of her own rules.

"Alice?" Lex said, knocking on the bathroom door.

There was no reply. She knocked again.

"Can I come in?" Lex asked, not waiting for a reply as she opened the door. Allison was sitting on the floor leaning up against the bathtub. Quietly, Lex sat next to her.

"Alice?" she said quietly, "are you ok?"

'That was a dumb thing to say,' she thought as she heard herself say it.

Allison wiped her nose with a tissue before replying quietly, "Yeah."

"Aiden told me about your patient...I'm really sorry..."

"What?" she cut her off. "Oh. Him. He was a complete psycho," she stated dismissively, "he was never going to get any better. I'm not upset about that."

"Then what?" she said, too easily dismissing the implications of her involvement in the hanging mental patient.

Allison looked Lex straight in the eyes. Lex noticed they were red and swollen.

"I'm pregnant," she said.

Lex found herself at a loss for words; stunned processing the reply of this young woman that she was so fond of...loved. Pregnant. A baby. That wasn't a piece of this puzzle at all. It certainly was not what she expected to hear. At the same time she was processing this, she also realized from Allison's demeanor that she was distressed as she sat silent, her face still wet from tears.

"I take it you guys weren't planning this," was all Lex could finally think to say.

Allison sat back, seeming more composed, more like the Allison she knew, responding:

"It's just, no, I mean, we knew we might have kids one day but, I don't know. I don't think I can do this."

'God, she is like me,' Lex thought.

"You know I'm screwed up, Lex...I can't have a baby. It's going to be all fucked up!" Allison exclaimed, "Remember when you told me that you were afraid that anyone with your genetics was going to be screwed up?"

"Well, that's not exactly what I said, but yes," Lex acknowledged.

"It's the same..."

"I doubt that," Lex cut her off.

"No. You don't even know," the young woman stated.

"Then tell me," Lex said cautiously. She knew this feeling well, knew that what she said, how she reacted, was going to make a difference, that it could influence the fate of her grandchild.

"You know I love Aiden, right? That I truly love him. And Avery, I would do anything for her. She is my heart. I couldn't imagine life without them. You know that, right?" Allison asked.

"Of course, I do," Lex said. And she meant it. There was such kindness to her, a vulnerability, a certain sincerity. Lex really did love this girl.

"I did it," Allison admitted, "I'm the one who set the fire, the one my parents died in."

If Allison expected a response of shock or repulsion, she wasn't going to get it from Lex. She sat calm, unaffected, just listening as Allison continued:

"I was five. My sister was seven. Holly Lee. My mom and dad worked late hours, so we always had a babysitter, sometimes an aunt, sometimes the girl down the street: Rose, her name was Rose. So, because they were home late, a lot of times they stayed over or would get picked up after my dad got home. He was always home first.

It's fuzzy, you know, the memories of that. I remember my dad chasing my aunt, and she locked herself in the bathroom, and it scared me. I didn't want to go to the bathroom, ever, and my mom thought there was something physically wrong. A doctor actually did a urinalysis. So anyway, there was that, and I remember coming around the corner once from the living room to the kitchen and seeing my dad hugging Rose, and she was crying, and I couldn't comprehend why. That piece is hazy to me.

"Anyway, like I said, the babysitters sometimes stayed over. I had two beds in my bedroom. So, one night, I woke up and I could hear my dad talking softly. He was in the other bed, facing the wall. I remember he had a blanket on; it was brown and had these weird different color stripes that made square designs.

"Please," he was whispering, "just let me do it. It will be ok."

He was talking to the babysitter, and she was crying a little, and I looked over at the doorway, and my sister was standing there. She saw the whole thing. Then my father saw her, and my sister ran to her room. I don't remember too much after that, but a few nights later, I looked out my bedroom window and saw my dad burying something in a garbage bag, and the next morning, my sister was gone. No one said anything, it was like nothing happened. Like she didn't exist. I was too scared to say anything. A couple days later, there was a candle in the living room. I was there alone. I tipped it over, just to see what would happen, but really, I think I wanted to hurt them. The fire spread so fast, the flames were so high, I panicked and ran out of the house.

Lex put her hand on Allison's knee as she spoke, looking at the White Rabbit tattoo and noticing for the first time the thin, horizontal scars covered by the tattoo. She seemed so small and vulnerable.

"I'm sorry, Alice," Lex told her sincerely. "You know that it makes sense for a little kid to be sad and scared, right?"

"Yes, of course," Allison replied, "I understand the psychology. To be honest, I didn't even remember it until much later. I just remember the incredibly overwhelming rage."

"Does anyone else know?" Lex inquired.

"The truth?" Allison replied, "Not the setting the fire part, but the rest, yes. I had therapy for it. Aiden knows."

"But not about setting the fire," Lex restated."No," Allison confirmed.

"Good," Lex told her.

Allison looked at her, confused.

"I'm going to tell you something, and I want you to really listen," Lex stated, commanded actually.

"What you did when you were a child doesn't matter now. Sometimes children only have themselves to save them. Don't tell anyone else. Ever. If you need to talk about this, talk to me. You hear me? What matters is who you are now. You are a beautiful, talented, loving young woman. Aiden loves you. Avery loves you. I love you. Our lives are better because you are here."

Lex heard Lilah in her own words as if she had taken over and spoke for her. "I am so sorry about what happened. I am so sorry about this," Lex touched the scars, "it's really fucked up and crazy, but it doesn't make you genetically defective. I promise you. Anyone would be lucky to have you as a mom."

"I'm scared, Lex," the young woman admitted.

"I know," Lex replied, validating her. "Me too. Bringing a child into the world is scary, and sometimes being a parent is terrifying."

"We're home!!" Avery's voice shouted from the hallway.

"Be right there!" Lex called back.

"Please don't tell him," Allison begged.

Lex looked her in the eyes and responded:

"Look, this is your choice. Only yours, right? You have to know I'm going to be biased, but I will not stand in the way of whatever you decide. I will keep this secret, even from my son. Because you are my daughter, and I love you. I want to remind you of one last thing though... Aiden is a wonderful father; you have a family that is here for you, and you're not alone."

She left Allison to get herself together before joining them. They ate pizza and talked about nothing late into the evening. Lex admitted to them that she knew she was interfering, pushing them to consider the preschool she picked out but still wanted them to choose that one anyway. Though she could not admit it to them, this was the school that Lex felt would be safe for Avery if she wasn't there to protect her.

As Lex got ready to leave them, she pulled at the small silver locket she always wore. It separated easily, and she handed it to Allison. Hugging her, she whispered:

"Lilah gave this to me before she died. To remind me to live," she told her.

"I love you both so much," Lex told them as she left them for what might be the last time: Now it was even more urgent that she get Jacob Stayley out of their lives for good.

Late in the night, as Aiden slept, Allison plugged the SD card into the computer and cued up the audio file. She listened to Lilah's voice:

'Lex, everything I should say, everything I should have said but never did swirls in my mind these days. I remember everything, you know: first conversation, first date, the way Pop was the only one who could call you Alexis, the

way you looked at me, and I knew you loved me, trusted us to have our son even though you were afraid.

I know how loved I feel, how I love you, how completely grateful I am for you, for us.

I remember when I first saw you. You asked me once why I pursued you; it seemed so out of the blue, and you never believed in coincidence. And I insisted it was random, fate. And you let it go knowing I was not being truthful. You accepted it. And I did pursue you.

It was a Saturday before finals in the library, and I was waiting impatiently to use a computer to finish writing my English term paper, at the last minute, of course. I saw you get up, saw my chance to take your spot. I only saw you from the back as you walked away, and I sat down and put my disk in, almost. But you hadn't cleared the screen, and your words hung in front of me. I almost cleared them, but curiosity got me, and I just had to read. I couldn't stop myself. I read it over and over and saved it to my disk. It wasn't right; I had to have it, though. I had to know you, know this person so different from me who in an instant made me feel the loneliness, the pain. It was so honest: You expressed and understood pain and chose to live.

I loved you immediately.

So, it is not my words that I want you to remember, Lex: It's yours. Because you need to remember this...

'Sometimes you fall...

.....sometimes it's just inevitable. You think that because it feels like it is worse than dying the most horrible death imaginable that it is. You believe it. You are laying there waiting for the dust to settle, and in the midst of it all, ironically, you sometimes laugh and "do life" and no-one notices any difference.

Though it can be quite painful, it is not necessarily a frightening place to be.

It is getting back up again that is frightening.

It is the fear of falling again, perhaps even harder, that is frightening.

It is the feeling of falling: the loss of control, the isolation, the aloneness.

It is rarely the fear of death. Death as a fear of the unknown is replaced with "It can't possibly be worse than this."

It is the insane search on the way down for something to grab onto to stop the fall...desperate, silent, over-powering: screaming, "HELP ME!"

It is the fear that next time you will feel nothing at all, that you will be in the Numb Zone where nothing feels like anything and where not getting up doesn't mean giving up...it means giving in.

It is the thought process during the fall. Swirling. Dizzying.

The letting go isn't about hurt to others...it is about the exhaustion of this constant battle.

You want people to understand, you don't want people to understand. It matters. It begins not to matter. And it feels like there is no way out, not even in death.

But...

Somewhere inside, you remember that it is the presence, not the words, that ultimately hold you to this earth, this life, your presence as someone who thinks, exists, loves and is loved, the presence and possibility of others that can love and hold you. The Safe Zones you create. Hopefully.

It is the granted times in-between the falling times that you have to build strength, begin a process of understanding and secure attachments to this life.

These are the things, if genuine, that are your meaning and are your reason to get back up. And if you are fortunate, these ties will hold you when you have fallen, though you may not recognize them or feel them. They will just exist.

You may barely make it. You may be laying in the imaginary dust saying and feeling, "I can't do it. I won't do it. I will not get up again."

But you do.

You get up and brush yourself off anyway. Knowing you may fall again. Maybe not as hard. Probably harder.

You get up and try to make this life more your life in the banged up, bruised hope that there will be no next time, that you will find your place and that will be enough.

You keep telling yourself that sometimes you fall simply so that you learn how not to.'

Allison could hear the sigh in Lilah's voice as she paused.

'Please, please, Lex, remember to be the person who wrote this, the one who always gets back up. Please be hopeful. Live. Love our son. Love Avery. Love yourself. Do this for me.

I love you forever and beyond.'

Hearing this caused Allison to smile through her tears.

20

At home, Lex paced her living room, agitated. Finally, the computer beeped, and the avatar appeared. It had evolved more, looked even more human with softer features.

"What can I do for you?" LilyQ asked. The voice was becoming more human, though the computerized sound still echoed in the speech.

"Who are you?" Lex demanded. "What do you want from me really?"

"I want to help you," LilyQ said calmly.

"That is such a lie," Lex replied, still pacing.

"What happened?" LilyQ asked.

"You tell me," Lex demanded.

"I don't understand your question," was the reply.

"I'm so mad right now!" Lex was shouting.

"What's wrong?" LilyQ asked.

"I can't tell you. Goddammit!" Lex said, knowing that if she said why she was mad, it could jeopardize her identity. "Just...dammit."

"Calm down," LilyQ demanded, "I need to know why you are mad."

"I should have walked away from you, from all of this."

"What is happening right now?"

'Was it a coincidence? Am I being played? C'mon, Lex, you are supposed to be good at this.'

"No. I should have given this more thought," Lex expressed, calming herself. "It's whatever."

"It's not," LilyQ stated. "Please tell me why you are upset so that I can help you."

"You can't help me. No one can." Lex stopped pacing. "You know what? Never mind. I don't have time for this right now."

Lex ended the transmission and destroyed the connection. Whatever this was, coincidence, whatever...there was no time to deal with it. She needed to calm down and refocus.

The overwhelming heat from the bathwater created a haze that steamed its way up the shower glass as Lex laid back in the water, a thick layer of bubbles covering her like a blanket. It was late, or early. The middle of the night was both and neither. She could hear her heart beating, pulsing in her ears.

'Don't do it, Lex.'

Allison's confession hurt. It was too close, too familiar, and Lex was too vulnerable. She needed to focus. She felt scattered. The hot water turned her skin pink. She could hear the bubbles popping around her. Still, she couldn't run from herself.

She felt ten years old and winter cold, when there is that moment when the beauty of Autumn turns lifeless, and a chill once welcome to relieve the heat of summer turns bone cold. This is where winter is not quite present but threatens at any moment, sometimes teasing with bitter wind and a first layer of frost. It is just prior to the first real snow of the season and late to provide a reflective blanket to protect the naked shivering trees. There is no time, just dark and light, and dark is forever long and light deceiving. Everything in that moment is dark and silent and frozen to death.

That was the feeling Lexi had, frozen to death as she watched the taxi in front of her father's car: Another Sunday, cold and dark. The taxi slowly led the way home. It shouldn't have. It was out of place, and Lexi was already in the nauseating survival space. There never seemed to be an end to it all, never seemed to be a cure for this illness. And yet, this was just fine with everyone else.

After all, why wouldn't it be ok for them to pull up to the house and see her stepfather with a toddler in his arms stagger into the house? What could possibly be unsafe about leaving children alone with him? But Lexi knew she and her sister would be left there: stray dogs at a high kill shelter.

He had set the toddler, still wearing his blue winter coat, on that blood red shag carpeted living room floor and was already in the kitchen at the stove, warming a can of baked beans, when they came through the front door. Her sister escaped quickly down into her room.

Lexi took the coat off the toddler as her step-father approached with a plate of beans in one hand. He sat down on the carpet, and leaning against a foot stool, put the plate on the floor between him and the child. He scooped a spoonful into his mouth and then into the toddler's mouth.

She took her bag of weekend clothes upstairs to her room and sighed in relief, having escaped the usual verbal assault. She sat on the side of her bed and kicked her shoes off, prying off one then the other with the opposite foot. The laces were in knots that she would never be able to untie. She could hear the phone ring and heard him answer, irritated. From the conversation, it must have been her mother, and she must have been trying to reach him for a while. He hung up the phone and then called to her:

"Lexi, come down here."

He wasn't shouting. His voice was raised only enough to ensure she heard him. She could have pretended not to hear, but that would have just delayed her interaction, and she just wanted to get through whatever humiliation there was going to be so she could shower and go to bed. As she made her way down the stairs, the absolute crippling tightness of anticipation eased a little. The waiting was so much worse, and she thought that at least they didn't come home to him passed out and the toddler sleeping in the toybox with cigarette ashes all over his lips.

The phone rang again, and she went to answer it.

"No, leave it," he told her and motioned her to him where he sat on the sofa.

She sat next to him, and the phone stopped ringing.

He reached for her face, and she flinched in anticipation of a slap but instead, he touched her hair. The phone started ringing again, and the toddler started crawling around. He touched her face.

"Pretty," he said.

Lexi was terrified and started to move away, but he grabbed her arm to keep her there. She could smell the alcohol: it was sweet but mixed with the smell of the sauce from the beans and old cigarettes. He reached forward and unsnapped the top button of her shirt. Lexi searched for an out.

"Aren't you gonna get the phone, it's probably Mom."

"Let it ring."

He tilted her chin up.

"Give me a kiss," he ordered, leaning in and placing his lips on hers. Lexi closed her eyes and waited for him to stop kissing her.

"No like this," he directed, "open your mouth."

She complied, and he kissed her harder, his hand on her chest. Lexi felt her heart beating faster, and her head was spinning. She could hear the *click click* of Mexican jumping beans that were in a little plastic box on the table. Everything went black.

The next thing that Lexi was conscious of was the scalding hot water running over her in the shower. She was choking from breathing it into her mouth and nose. She was shaking and cold, though the water was scalding her skin.

'I gotta get out of here,' the panic told her.

Lexi jumped out of the shower. The bathroom door was open, and her clothes were in a pile in the hallway. She put on her shirt without drying. It clung to her skin. She picked up her jeans to put them on. They were still zipped and buttoned, and the macramé belt was still knotted around them though the belt loops were ripped. As she pulled them on, she felt a throbbing pain.

Lexi felt panic cry out in her throat, but she swallowed it back.

'Run, Lexi,' she thought. But what difference did it make now?

She didn't know time, just darkness and naked cold. The shiver deep in her was tight and nauseating, but only her hair felt cold: it was wet from the shower that should have stopped the shaking.

'I've gotta to get out of here,' swirled in her brain, though her voice said:

"I have to go check my homework with my friend."

He barely acknowledged her as she walked out of the house with no coat and her hair wet and unbrushed.

Out in the darkness, the person taking the steps down the driveway wasn't her; and yet it was.

'What will I say? What should I do?'

The moonlight reflected on the frost, casting an eerie light on the homes, on the trees. She could hear the crackle of her steps in the dark silence and the thump of her heart loud in her head. She walked up to the neighbor's house and knocked. Nothing. A sharp cold zap of electric panic zipped through her chest.

She knocked again. No one was home. Lexi's brain started hurting.

'Somebody help me.'

She turned and walked in the silent darkness down the street in the other direction. She was afraid to say anything, afraid to make noise, afraid night might devour her. As she walked, she tried to calculate how much time she had before being gone was being gone too long. She was no longer aware of her body, her skin or her steps or the pace, just that she was somewhere else. Another friend's house whose mom was a police officer.

"I need to call my mom," she told her.

There was no past, no future, just that moment sitting at her friend's kitchen table. And as she started to tell her mom, she can only say these words:

"He kissed me..." and she heard her voice stop. And there was dead silence. And she heard the words across a chasm:

"Where are your brother and sister?"

"At home."

"You left them there?" her mother said, and then: "What do you want me to do?"

"Come home."

She was no longer shivering. She was nothing...a part of the dark chill and eerie silence of night.

She heard her mother, kind and apologetic and a victim, she could hear it in her voice as she talked to her friend's mom. There would be no help, no police to fix this. Lexi shut down.

'I am not like her. I am not a victim,' she thought, hearing her mother's words in the car ride home:

"Why did you go to a neighbor's house? Do you know what they think of me now? Do you know how embarrassing that was?"

Her voice seemed far away. Lexi wasn't listening anyway. She was now a part of the darkness; the dead frosted trees that they were passing.

'I am nothing...'

Lex watched the tiny bubbles pop one by one in her hand, the pain swirling fresh as if she was still a child. She held the blade of her knife against her arm.

'Don't do it, Lex.'

She made a little cut. She watched the small trail of blood run down her arm, turning the bubbles red. It was, for a moment, satisfying. At least she could feel something, and it was enough.

She waited until blood no longer slipped from the fresh wound before getting out of the tub. Once dressed, she played absently with the dog, throwing the ball over and over until the dog tired out and the first light of dawn appeared across the horizon. She checked the security cameras. No Jacob. This was her window. It was time to shake the beehive.

"I'm safe, up high, nothing can touch me..." -Pink

21

The morning sun rose slowly, casting fractured light through the morning haze. Lex tried not to let the silence of the slow passing moments get to her as she sat outside of his hotel, watching, waiting for him to leave. As morning slipped into early afternoon, the haze burned away revealing the beautiful blue that signified the best of California. 1p.m. Finally, he emerged, skipping down the stairs and speeding away. Lex's hands were shaking, and she struggled momentarily putting on gloves.

'You can do this.'

She walked in the shadow of the buildings, avoiding the storefront security monitors. She waited for a young couple to make their way down the street before quickly taking the stairs and breaking into Jacob's room.

Sighing in relief, Lex made her way to the wall. One by one, she removed the pictures and burned them completely in a trash can. She pulled out the black ash remnants, scattering them on the floor just beneath where they were hanging. From her pocket, she pulled out a single playing card. An *Uno* wild card. She taped it to the wall.

"Uno asshole," she said out loud and exited quickly.

Across town, Jacob sat in a café eating. He watched his young waitress as she chatted with another customer, sizing her up: beautiful and well-groomed, young. Probably an actress. Naima. She had served him several times. She might be just what he needed: So polite..."Yes, sir, no sir, thank you"...music to his ears.

She brought him his check.

"What time you off, sweetheart?" he asked her with a smile.

She giggled, "Oh, Jake, wouldn't you just like to know."

"I would indeed. Seriously, girl, don't leave me hangin', let me take you out."

The young woman looked around to make sure her boss couldn't hear her.

"I'm off at five," she told him quietly.

"I'll be here then," he told her and winked.

'About time,' he thought to himself. He usually never worked that hard, but she was something special, something he could work with. His mind wandered to everything he wanted to do with her, to her. He thought about the long game. She was a keeper, that one.

He was still daydreaming about the girl when he got back to his room, but reality hit hard when he saw his burned memories and the Uno wildcard taped in their place.

They had very few possessions as children: this was Melissa's favorite. No one could know that, and it hit him: It was *her.* And it made sense now why she and Avery never went anywhere. How long had she been playing him? Blinding rage consumed him.

He yelled incoherently as he ripped the card off the wall. He was going to kill Alexis Vance, stuff that card down her throat and then he was going to take Avery from whomever had her, and he would kill them too, kill everyone in his way.

He peeled out of the hotel driveway.

Lex paced her living room, watching the surveillance camera images. She felt the anxiety all the way to her fingertips. She hated confrontation. This would definitely be confrontation. She thought again about calling the police as she walked back and forth. She thought about trying to strangle her stepfather in a confrontation, how he had given her a good, visible black eye. She thought about how she was told to forgive him because his brother had just died in a drug deal gone bad. She thought about how the police, again, did nothing.

"It doesn't hurt."

She watched the skies darken and rain begin to fall. She thought about the risk as her heart raced in anticipation. She told herself to relax. This was well planned. The gun was in the car. The keys were in the ignition, shopping bags in the back seat. He just had to take the bait. He would. She knew him well enough now: What a twisted, predictable fuck.

Finally, there he was, slowly pulling up to the curb a block away. She stared at his parked car for a while, waiting to leave, cursing the slow-moving time. If she left right away, it would be too obvious, too planned.

'Don't do it, Lex.'

"It's too late," she said out loud to the voice in her head as she got into her car.

She watched him in her rear-view mirror, back a few car lengths. If she wasn't so scared, she would have congratulated herself for knowing him so well. Darkness enveloped the horizon through the steady rain. She took her time on the streets, on the freeway, stopping at several well-lit and populated stores, then another long street, back on the freeway, making stops, 'running errands,' careful not to let on that she knew he was following, careful not to let the fear show.

Lex's mind flashed to Lilah:

"This road you are on...you know where it leads. It's not who you are."

'Oh, Lilah...Lilah, I wish it was true. I made a mess of things.'

Finally, Lex pulled into the Food 4 Less parking lot, driving to a far corner to park. There was no surveillance and very little light. And no one ever shopped past 9 p.m. here. She parked and sat quietly, pretending to pull things out of her purse as she put on latex gloves. She got out of the car and opened the back door. Reaching for an empty grocery bag, she heard him quickly approach from behind her. Too quickly. She had underestimated his urgency; she thought he would be more cautious, not calculating that blind rage would abolish any sense of self control.

He grabbed her right arm and twisted her around. She heard it snap and felt the sharp pain jolt through her arm. As he spun her around, she raised the gun with her left hand. He released her and began slowly backing up. He had underestimated her as well.

They stood silent. Lex had thought many times of what she might say to this man who threatened her family, but nothing came. This wasn't exactly the plan.

She just stared at him. Jacob stared back.

'Shoot him!' she thought.

She was frozen, and he saw it: fear.

She had pictured that she would walk past him on the way into the market and either he would A: try to grab her then or B: he would allow her to shop and he would grab her on the way back to her car. Either way, she figured he would try to force her into his trunk. Lex had gambled that quick death was not what Jacob had planned, that when he made his move she would make hers, pull the gun, and get him into his own trunk. Then she would drive him to the wash up the road, set his car on fire and send it into the ravine. The noise and chaos would allow her to slip unnoticed back to her car.

'Shoot him!'

Jacob smiled as old words came back to haunt her:

'What if she had pulled the trigger and shot you?'

'She wouldn't have.'

'You don't know that. Everyone's life would be ruined.'

'There is no way she would shoot me. She's too scared.'

Jacob confidently took a step forward but stopped abruptly: Her eyes changed.

Lex pulled the trigger and fell back against the car, not used to the recoil in her left hand. If she had the use of her right hand to steady it, she would have been more accurate, but it hit, nonetheless.

Jacob stood a moment in disbelief. A searing painful sensation tore at his right side. He felt himself fall to his knees.

"You shot me!" he yelled in disbelief.

The gun shook in Lex's hand. Jacob' s voice was different than she imagined, deeper, a bit southern, not like Melissa's; hers was more refined. She shook her head in shock.

"Damn," she said calmly, "I did."

And he was still alive, but the amount of blood told her that it probably wouldn't be for long. He started dragging himself to his car as it began to rain a bit harder.

'Run, Lexi...'

She tossed the gun in a shopping bag and ran over to a storm drain. The grate was heavier to lift with one hand, and she struggled with it, looking around for witnesses.

Jacob was pulling open his driver's side door.

"Fuck!" she said aloud, the grate finally giving. She tossed the bag in and heard it hit the shallow water. Then she rolled the gloves together and tossed them in. She ran to her car and started the engine. So did he.

She had wanted him alive for a few minutes: alive to suffer but not for long enough to do more than contemplate his death. This was an execution. Jacob dragging himself to his own car was the opposite of that; not only did he not die, now he was racing towards her. Still very much alive. Lex hit the gas and entered the freeway with Jacob close behind.

'Reckless...'

22

A low, steady buzz crept through the dark haze with an image of an old, ominous school room, one from the 1970's with individual grey metal pocket desks: the kind with an attached thin seat and a desktop that could be lifted so that school books, paper, crayons and other school supplies could be easily stored.

The floor tiles gleamed white-gray and speckled in rows of 12-by-12-inch squares, dirty and worn, chipped in some places, gouged in others and scuffed. Walls that were thick with layers of cold light green paint were covered in art projects. Students sat in rows as ghosts out of time facing a chalkboard filled with numbers, maybe letters, but jumbled and indistinguishable as anything of value.

The buzz was overhead, from the rows of inset long fluorescent bulbs. Though there might have been conversation, from children, from a teacher, it was less than a mumble...maybe from another room, maybe a hallway, but not in this room, and anyway, it was drowned out by that buzz and by the *click, click, click* of the second hand of the round clock as it inched closer 3 p.m.

Click, click, click.

Her heart pounded three times as fast, every third beat in sync with the sensation of each click. Soon, the safety of nothingness would once again be replaced with drowning terror of what might be waiting at home. She could feel the nausea inside like an ache or a bruise against her jeans, her shirt.

Click, click, click.

Her mind searched for some comfort.

'I know it's Tuesday, I know she is off...is she? She'll be home. She'll be home.'

There was no Tuesday, not today. No matter the desperate convincing.

'Maybe something happened, and Mom is not working today. She will be there when I get home.'

It had happened before, so maybe.

This ritual was the only thing that calmed the intense shaking inside; the swirling, the drowning completely paralyzing her. If a teacher, if anyone had called out to her, she wouldn't know. Not now, not with the time dwindling.

Click, click, click.

'Come on, stop being crazy,' she pleaded.

Click, click, click.

And then the shrill ring...

Lex woke, startled and sweating.

"Jesus," she said out loud in the unfamiliar hospital room: The bright, buzzing light overhead, the green walls, the tile floors. The hospital bed. Everything rushed into her like the blow back from an explosion.

She was still alive.

'Reckless.'

"How do you feel?" came a voice.

"I don't know. Drugged," she answered slowly, still groggy.

She sat up, and a sharp pain shot through her chest, stopping her fast. She sucked in her breath and took inventory of her injuries; her right wrist and arm now properly wrapped, her left arm attached to an IV plugged into her at the wrist, the rest of her hand empty...

"What the hell?!" Lex exclaimed.

"You were in a car accident..."

"Where are my rings?" she demanded.

"Do you remember any..."

"Where are my fucking wedding rings!!?" she yelled attempting to jump off the bed.

Lex felt panic rise and a swirling instability as the hot thump of her heartbeat loomed in her throat. She heard the words, distant but from her. She thought she heard herself say, "I'll fucking kill you." Then everything went warm and black...

23

D etective Stan Dixon leaned against the wall of the hospital corridor, drinking bottled water. He was a patient man, a characteristic that served him well over the years. As he slowly and methodically sipped water, he watched his partner pace. Erin Hereford was completely the opposite, a baby with her eight months' experience only, to his twenty-two years: his punishment for pissing off the lieutenant at a press conference. She paced, chewed gum and, to his annoyance, blew and popped bubbles constantly.

"Your jaw is going to break," he stated, sarcastically.

She stopped. "When are we going to talk to this woman? We've been waiting forever."

"When we are given permission," he replied quietly.

"Jesus already," the young detective said, rolling her eyes. "We should just go in there. This is ridiculous."

"Relax. The questions will be the same, now or later. Why don't you just appreciate the downtime?" he asked her.

"Because, we could be out doing our job, not waiting around to ask questions about a traffic accident. We should be out doing real work," she replied impatiently.

"This is real work," Detective Dixon said calmly, "investigating traffic accidents, doing paperwork, this is the job," he stated more to annoy her than express the fact.

It drove him crazy to babysit, but he didn't let on; he never would. This was a personal attack, and he would not allow it to get the better of him. Besides, he liked the downtime. Three years left. He wanted to lay low.

Time passed slowly as they watched people come and go from the room. He figured the woman was awake or at least conscious based on the type of staff now entering. They had arrived just minutes too late yesterday, hitting the doorway as the woman was being scooped off the floor, sedated, and then arms secured to the bed rails, 'for her own protection' the doctor told him, but he had heard her yell "I'll fucking kill you" before passing out, and he knew that really, it was the staff that was being protected.

"The on-call therapist is going to assess her," a young doctor offered as he exited the room. "Once she clears her, she's all yours."

"Finally," the young detective commented.

"C'mon," Dixon said, motioning down the hall. "Let's get some fresh air." And then to the doctor: "So, about an hour then?"

The doctor nodded.

"Wha..?" Erin began.

"It's rounding," Dixon explained as they walked down the hall. "It will be at least that before they get to her."

Erin rolled her eyes responding, "Fine."

24

Lex dozed on and off in a soft drug haze. Though she wasn't quite sure of the time or the day, she was actually happy to be drugged, it excused her from dealing with anyone. She assumed that Jacob was dead because, though she was secured to the bed by the wrists, they weren't handcuffs, and she noticed her wedding rings had been secured back to their proper place, which was probably Allison's doing.

Those drug-induced dreams, though, they pierced her as if she were both a voodoo doll and its victim. The familiar images and memories denied that were virtually inescapable under the influence haunted her somewhere deep in her soul and they stayed with her in consciousness like a thick slow lifting fog.

"When are you going to untie me?" she asked, demanded really, of the woman checking the monitor opposite her bed.

She needed desperately to walk away and preoccupy her mind. If she could get out and back to her routine, back to Avery and the dog. And to 'her life.' Had she shut the game down properly? Had Jacob really died? How much time has passed? She needed to get to a computer to either start or stop the cascade of information from 'appearing.' She needed to get to the gun…

'*Reckless*'

And overconfident. This stupid resurgence of everything horrible in her childhood was making mistakes.

"Now," came a voice from the door.

A familiar voice. Lex smiled.

"Allison, thank God," Lex sighed, relieved.

The nurse nodded a hello to the women.

"I'm good here," she told the nurse.

"Sure, Dr. Leighton," she responded, leaving the two to talk.

Allison began undoing the wrist restraints.

"I'm so sorry," she told her as she released the restraints. "It's protocol when a patient is overly agitated. Do you remember what happened?"

"No," Lex lied.

"The attending said that when you first woke up, you were hysterical, yelling about your wedding rings. He said you almost bit him."

"Really? "she asked cautiously as she rubbed her wrist. "My God, I'm so sorry. Did I bite him?"

She knew she didn't. In fact, she knew she didn't even lunge at him.

'*Prick*,' she thought.

"No," Allison said, hugging her.

"Where is that son of mine?" Lex inquired.

"With Avery. How are you feeling?"

"Better...major headache, was I really that out of control?" Lex responded.

Allison sat on the bed.

"What do you remember?"

"No...yes, maybe? I kind of remember waking up, but that's all. It's really foggy. Are you analyzing me?" she answered.

Allison was definitely right to be suspicious, and Lex wondered if she would one day be the one to see through all of this. And she wondered what that would mean.

"Sort of," she replied. "You know I can't help it. Someone else will be coming to talk to you, though. And the police..."

"The police? Why?" She began to shift uncomfortably.

"Well let's see...you were almost killed by some maniac," Allison answered with quiet sarcasm.

"Oh."

Lex's mind wandered back to that moment as the haze lifted a bit, and she remembered hitting the brakes. Yes, she was almost killed. Twice. And it was all on her. She was the maniac. How ironic.

"Lex, what happened?" Allison asked hesitantly.

"I think I cut him off...her. No, definitely a him. I cut him off. I guess I pissed him off. Is he ok?" Lex could feel the panic rise quickly, remembering what just one word from that 'him' would mean to the rest of her life if he had indeed survived. She swallowed it back.

"No, he didn't make it," Allison told her solemnly.

Lex laid back and sighed in relief but caught herself quickly. Allison's inquisitive look prompted her to speak.

"I don't know, Alice, I feel relieved. Is that horrible of me?"

"Do you think it is?" Allison asked, answering Lex's question with a question.

"Honestly, I don't know," Lex again lied.

"Well, I would think that maybe you thought you were going to die," Allison said.

The statement seemed to Lex more like she was feeding her an answer than making a guess. She was about to agree with her when someone knocked lightly and partially entered: A detective, she guessed, from the way he was dressed.

"If we could have a moment?" the man said.

Allison looked at Lex for approval. She nodded, adding quicky:

"Can I use your phone?"

Allison handed it to her casually.

"I'll be back a bit later," she told Lex, rising from the bed, "I told Aiden about the baby."

"Good," Lex responded.

Allison passed by the detectives, telling them quietly: "Not too long. I'm not quite sure she knows what she is saying yet."

As she walked down the hall, the words from the accident site police officer echoed in her head:

"The witnesses said she just stopped, slammed on her brakes."

Allison knew there was more. What was "the more?" She bit her lower lip as she always did when she was worried. And she was worried. That sigh of relief was so...relieved. It wasn't an odd response, it wasn't abnormal. It was different. She couldn't put her finger on it. Maybe she didn't want to. She shook the thought away and called Aiden to give him an update.

In the hospital room, that exact thought weighed on Detective Dixon's mind as he and Detective Hereford approached the slight, semi-bandaged woman. Instantly, it amused him that she was the cause of the commotion a day earlier. This slight creature that had to be restrained for 'hospital staff safety' couldn't be more than five-foot three, maybe 115 pounds.

"Good afternoon," his partner said, still chewing gum, "I'm Detective Hereford, and this is Detective Dixon. We need to ask you a few questions about your accident."

Lex looked up from the phone but continued to hold her thumb on the black portal screen as she lowered it to her side.

'Fuck hurry up,' she thought, hoping the triggers would complete before anyone noticed.

She looked from one detective to the other and said nothing.

"Ok, well then," Detective Hereford began, "What was your relationship with Eric Matthews..."

"Why don't we start from the beginning," Detective Dixon interrupted, "in your words."

Lex turned her gaze again from one to the other.

"I'm not sure really...it's a little fuzzy."

She surmised that their silence was a cue to continue and noticed that the woman was beginning to take an interest in the phone.

"I was driving...I switched lanes. The next thing I knew, this car came up next to me and the guy driving started yelling. I turned away to ignore him and continue driving and the next thing I knew, he bumped the side of my car. It scared me, you know, and I looked back and this guy,

I don't know, he looked crazy mad. So, I sped up to get away from him. The rest you know."

"Where were you headed?" Detective Hereford asked.

"Home," Lex answered.

Detective Dixon shot the young detective an annoyed look and continued with his questions:

"What exactly did Mr. Matthews say to you?"

"Mr. Matthews is...was the guy chasing me?" Lex asked uncomfortably.

He nodded yes.

"I have no idea. My windows were up, I had music on. Like I said, he seemed to be yelling, he seemed mad. I didn't think it was in my best interest to stop and have a conversation, you know?"

The phone gave a short quiet buzz, indicating success.

"Did you need to get that?" Detective Hereford asked, wanting to know what Lex was doing with the phone.

"No," Lex replied, turning her hand just enough so that the detective, who thought she was being stealth, could see her phone and the normal texting screen, "I was just checking on my dog."

Detective Dixon continued his questioning:

"Have you seen him before?"

"No," Lex told him, shifting unconsciously.

"Are you sure?"

"I said no already. Look, did I do something wrong? I mean I know I was speeding, but," she paused thinking of her conversation with Allison, "I really thought I was going to die."

"So, you were in fear for your life," Detective Hereford stated.

"Yes."

"But you had no history with this man."

"No," Lex confirmed. "I think I just cut him off, and he snapped or something. But that look in his eyes..." she shuddered, "it was terrifying."

Lex was being honest, his look was terrifying, just for a different reason.

Detective Dixon took over:

"A witness, a couple of them actually, made statements that you slammed on your brakes prior to the accident."

"I don't remember," Lex easily lied.

She knew better. Keep it short and simple. Don't dig a hole. She thought back to Aiden as a child, weaving elaborate lies when caught doing something he wasn't supposed to. She pictured Lilah engaging with him patiently, letting him dig himself in deeper while Lex was relegated to the background because Lex 'would just laugh and not take it seriously.' And Lilah was right, of course. Lex found this amusing.

"Ms. Vance..."

"Mrs.," Lex corrected.

Detective Hereford reviewed her notes.

"I'm sorry, I thought your wife had passed..."

"Yes," Lex stated, "it's 'til death do you part."

They both just looked at her.

"I'm not dead," Lex stated, matter-of-fact.

Detective Hereford just stared at her.

"I see. Ok," Detective Dixon said finally, "I apologize."

Lex was beginning to feel nervous. The medication was wearing off, causing her to grow impatient and irritable. And uncomfortable. She felt trapped, caged. How badly she would have liked to grab that gum chewing child detective by the hair and ram her face into the wall...

"I'm sorry," she said finally. "Look, I'm really tired, and I don't really remember anything else..."

"Sure, sure," he told her, "good enough."

He placed his business card on the side tray, adding, "Thank you for your time. If you think of anything else, please give us a call."

He motioned to his partner, and they turned to leave.

"I will," she called after them, then quickly turned back to the phone, confirming that Jacob Staley had been erased.

As they walked into the hallway, Detective Dixon muttered to himself:

"Here it comes..."

"Good enough?" Detective Hereford shot. "Are you kidding? We waited hours for that conversation, and you're just...done? It didn't bother you that she was texting someone the whole time we were there?"

He stopped her.

"Erin what do you think?"

The young detective replied with her observations:

"That it doesn't make sense, even in Los Angeles, for someone to just randomly chase someone down for no reason. And that woman was very cautious and short with her answers, like she was on the stand or something. That she was calm but when she looked at me, I felt like she wanted to rip my head off."

"What else?" he encouraged.

"What do you mean?" she asked.

He elaborated on his previous question:

"What else did you see?"

She shrugged.

"Ok, let's think it through. Beyond the statement, what do you see?"

"Someone banged-up from a car accident," Erin offered.

They walked slowly down the hall.

"Tell me about the accident," Dixon inquired.

"Well, the car hit from behind, sending the SUV into a spin, where it finally hit the wall."

"And the airbags?"

"All deployed, front and side," Erin Hereford reported.

"So, what about her injuries?"

"Bruises, mostly from the airbags and the seatbelt. Cracked ribs. A few cuts, probably from the glass shattering. Concussion. A broken arm."

Detective Dixon calmly continued to pose questions to the young detective, taking responsibility to teach her all of the nuances of detective work that could not be learned from a classroom. He knew the instinct was there, and if he nurtured it, she might just be a good detective one day. One day. Maybe not in his remaining three years.

"Here is what I see," he said, finally exhausted from leading the 'child' detective. "Details. Broken arm. All of the injuries are consistent with the crash and the airbags. Except that break. Is it possible? Sure. The impact was severe. But the medical report says it is a spiral fracture. That did not happen in an accident. Also, the witnesses. Their stories were consistent. All accounts have her slamming on her brakes. Why do that, and is it relevant? Right now, our 'victim' says she can't remember much, so we may not get anywhere with that. For now."

"I don't believe her, it doesn't feel right," Detective Hereford commented.

"So, we'll follow what we have for now. Let's find out who these people are," he replied.

The young detective agreed. Now, it was interesting.

25

The detectives' floor was dreary...décor from the '60s, only updated with newer furniture, and finally, newer computers, though some of the 'new' of the newer computers was questionable. Dixon often noted that the floor looked almost the same as his first day many, many years ago. The forensics lab, by contrast, was high tech, the best equipment affordable, and that was what really mattered: most of the time, they were only as good as the evidence they collected.

He didn't have much use for a computer: He could use it, sure, but he never quite got used to doing much more than a basic search. This was mostly because it was so slow. He was an Apple guy actually and liked to use his iPad and iPhone...devices that were a bit more user-friendly. Generally, he went to the lab if he really need-ed something, or to a computer tech because what they could do in minutes often took him hours...and wasn't that what they were there for anyway?

He sent Detective Hereford down to the coroner's office to hopefully push up the autopsy timeline. She wouldn't accomplish this with charm, but she had a way of talking people into a corner, and they would find that their only way out was to do as she asked. That was a great asset when he wasn't the person in the corner.

"Marcus, did you run the background checks for me?" he asked.

"Sure did. Didn't you get my email?" the IT tech responded.

"Didn't I say text me? I don't check email."

"You should," Marcus said to himself under his breath.

"So, what do you have?" Dixon asked.

Marcus pulled up the profiles.

"These are regular people, man. Seriously."

"Let me see." Detective Dixon motioned for him to move out of his way.

He scrolled through the data. It was true. These were regular people: the doctors, their child. A first wife who died tragically of an overdose. He paused on Alexis Vance and read carefully through what little was available: Computer Programmer, last position in security. Wife died of cancer. These were things they already knew.

"Hey, Marcus, can we see financial information?" he asked.

"Like bank accounts? Sure." Marcus replied, typing on the keyboard.

"I can't interpret any of this," the detective scowled. What had happened to the simple bank account number, amount of money, cancelled checks? This was lines of data that seemed convoluted.

Marcus took over:

"Well, there is a life insurance transfer every month... see? Here," he pointed. "This is from her late wife. It looks like it is paying out about two million dollars..."

"That seems excessive," Dixon stated.

"No, not really. Not anymore. The wife worked for a large drug company; she was pretty high up. There's also a pension," Marcus explained.

"Hmm, what else?" the detective asked, staring at the data but relying on the IT tech's interpretation.

Marcus continued scrolling:

"Well, this right here, these are from an investment company. It looks like she makes good decisions...maybe I should hit her up for advice," the young technician commented absently. "And here, this is private equity. Property Management. All legitimate."

Marcus scrolled past the financial information.

"Here is something, though. Well, not something. Nothing actually. Alexis Vance is missing from the network for a substantial time. No Facebook, Twitter, Instagram, no real paper trail."

"I don't have a Facebook," Dixon stated.

Marcus continued:

"Right, but we can still look up basic information about you, birth certificate, social security number. There are certain consistent data elements, kind of an electronic signature that almost everyone has now."

"I don't get it," he commented.

"Well, it's just inconsistent," the IT tech explained, "there are holes. Maybe the nature of someone who works in cyber security, because they are pretty paranoid actually, it's just inconsistent. Prints and DNA still in progress, nothing major yet. Printed for a firearm. A Chiappa Rhino DS60. Would have had to have been modified to a single shot to be registered in California."

Detective Dixon switched his focus. "What about Eric Matthews?"

"Prints and DNA?" Marcus asked. "We haven't received it yet. We'll get that officially when the autopsy is done."

"Detective Hereford is on that," the detective commented.

"Well, that will move things along," Marcus stated sarcastically.

"Anything else on him?" Dixon asked, ignoring the comment.

"I haven't started that yet, and before you say anything, I'm backed up for a week, but yes, I will do it as soon as I can. Basic search, there is nothing that you do not know...hotel, rental car. When I get the prints, I can run something more," Marcus told him as he turned back to his computer

"Ok, let me know," the detective said, walking away.

"Yeah, I'll send you an email," Marcus called out after him.

26

"Mom, what would you like to eat?" Aiden called out from Lex's kitchen.

"Nothing, I'm not hungry," she called back from the living room.

She had been home for half a day, and already, Aiden had asked twice. He came into the living room. The dog followed, passing him and jumping onto the sofa.

"Hey, careful," Aiden said, pushing the dog away from her.

"Aiden, I'm fine. The dog isn't going to break me, it's ok. You can go home now," she told him.

"No way," he replied quickly, "I'm staying here tonight. You cannot be here alone."

"Seriously?" Lex asked, trying not to sound annoyed or ungrateful.

"Seriously," he answered. "Now, what do you want to eat?"

"Nothing," Lex replied, pulling a blanket up around her shoulders.

"See, now that doesn't inspire me to leave," he told her.

Lex rolled her eyes. "Ok, Lilah," she said sarcastically.

"Exactly. Mom would never stand for this," he shot back.

That was an understatement. Lilah nearly brought in a home visit nurse when Lex broke her leg snowboarding and Lilah had to return to work. Being honest, Lex admitted to herself that it was nice to have Aiden there. They had spent so little time together alone lately. She just needed him gone so that she could work.

"Jello," she told him, "shots. With vodka."

"And Jello it is..." he said, walking back to the kitchen.

"Honey," she called after him, resigned, "let's order something. You don't need to cook."

As they ate, Lex took the opportunity to discuss more personal items.

"So...a baby, huh?" she asked.

"Aww, she told you?" he seemed disappointed.

"Well, yeah, at the hospital," Lex told him. "She talks to me."

"I was going to wait until you were feeling better," he complained.

"Hmm. And I guess Alice thought it would 'make' me feel better," she answered.

"And did it?" he asked.

"Of course. I am so happy for you guys. And for Avery. She is going to be so excited," Lex replied.

"You think so? I'm worried that she will feel displaced," he shared.

"Ha! That's funny," she laughed at him, but saw he was serious.

"Don't overthink it," she added. "There are brothers and sisters everywhere, and they survive the jealousy and the rivalry. You were jealous when we got Cal, remember?"

"Cal was a dog," he commented.

"Yes, and you were jealous because every day, you went to school, and the dog went to Grandpa Al's," Lex reminded him.

"I don't remember that," he teased, causing her to laugh.

Lex reached across the table and covered his hand with hers, telling him:

"She's going to be great. This will be good for her, just like Alice is good for her."

Lex yawned and stood slowly.

"So, don't mess it up," she kissed the top of his head. "I'm going to go to bed."

"Mom?" he called after her, "I love you."

"Love you, too," she replied.

Aiden sat back on the sofa and turned on the TV. He didn't like this one bit. It wasn't the part where his mother was nearly killed, of course, that was bad. It was his mother's reaction, which might have been the concussion, it was only a few days ago, but he observed the same reaction from her when Melissa died: mechanical, distant. At the time, he attributed it to Lilah's illness. But this was eerily similar. And something else bothered him: His mother was very set in her opinions, headstrong, but twice now, when she made a sudden 180, something went terribly wrong: First when she agreed that Melissa should be able to return to caring for Avery and now, all of a sudden, pre-school was a good idea. And he couldn't get himself to accept it, but really down deep, he did believe that she had slammed on the brakes of the SUV.

He called Allison to check in. She was convinced of coincidence, and that it wasn't true and logically explained it all away as nothing. It was dark, the witnesses would have seen the tires possibly locked up once the car hit her. No way his mother slammed on the brakes, she was trying to get away. She believed this. She made him want to believe it. He just didn't.

Across town, Detective Dixon had settled in for the night. He had a good dinner with his wife, and they were now watching TV. He saw his phone light up. It was Detective Hereford.

'I'm not answering it,' he thought, but answered anyway.

"Stan, I've got something!" she almost shouted.

If only he was still that excited about the work.

"Did you hear me?" she asked.

"Yes," he said quietly, excusing himself from the living room. "Let's hear it."

"Eric Matthews wasn't just crushed in the accident. He was shot. And guess what with?" she wasn't really asking him, "A Chiappa Rhino 60DS. And guess who owns one?"

"Did you get a search warrant?" he asked, his interest increasing.

"Working on it now," she responded. "She must have shot him and..."

"Stop," Dixon told her, "Let's theorize if we recover a weapon and if the ballistics match."

"Oh, they will," she stated.

As he finished his conversation with his overly eager partner, he returned to the living room.

"Anything important?" his wife asked.

"A lead on a case; it'll wait until tomorrow," he explained.

"Good," she told him, motioning for him to sit with her.

His gut told him that the gun registered to her, if she had it, would not be a match. He believed that she shot him; experience told him a gunshot and an accident were very rarely an accident. But something about the caution in Alexis Vance's demeanor as they spoke told him she was one step ahead of them.

He joined his wife, cuddling her in his arms, losing himself in the TV show.

'Three more years...'

27

The knock came right on cue as per the call asking if she was available for more questions, asking if she owned a gun, and she agreed. Lex greeted the detectives and their team as Aiden came up behind her.

"I don't like this. That man was shot...they want your gun," he whispered to her, "We should have called our attorney."

"Yeah, son," she responded just as quietly, "because I went out, found this person, shot him and then got into a car accident with him. I didn't shoot anyone, and they know it, otherwise the warrant would be to arrest me. Just because I own a similar gun doesn't mean they can arrest me. They better not break my stuff."

"Detectives...come on in," Lex told them calmly.

"We have a warrant to search your home for ammunition and a revolver, specifically a Chiappa Rhino 60DS."

Detective Dixon watched the woman's response. She just smiled confidently.

"Of course you do," she responded.

"I don't understand this," Aiden said angrily. "My God, she is the victim. What is your problem?"

"Son," she stopped him and then turned to Detective Dixon, "just doing your job, right? So, do you actually have more questions for me or are you just searching?"

She was toying with him, the detective surmised. Confident. What they were looking for was definitely not here. Regardless, they were there to tie up a lead. He followed her as she led him through her home. The living room was clean but littered with toys...cars, dolls, a toy doctor kit. The coffee table had a stack of coloring books and crayons. Normal, familial. iPad, TV remote, keyboard, video game controllers. Television mounted over a fireplace.

"Nice," he caught himself saying.

She led him to a room right off the living room. A bedroom. From the pictures, from the clothes hanging on hooks, he figured it must be hers. He was led to what looked like a narrow antique vanity. There were various trinkets, a little Chinese statue, a cloisonné vase and small animals. A candle. What was most interesting, though, was what was in the locked glass case.

Various knives, perhaps collectibles: a switch blade, totally illegal, a butterfly knife, the same, throwing stars, a couple of oddly shaped blades on stands, one he recognized from a movie. And a gun.

Lex took a key from her pocket.

"This is what you were looking for?" she asked, opening the case slowly.

There it was on a stand, the exact gun that was registered to her. The exact model that had shot Eric Matthews. But it wasn't THE gun, and he knew it. It was stunning, intricately designed. Flat black steel with gold detail. Pieces of ivory on the barrel.

She reached for it.

"No. Don't," Detective Dixon ordered.

He motioned to one of his fellow officers to confiscate it.

"My mother had that made for her," Aiden stated.

"Been fired?" he asked.

"Yes, years ago. And repaired and cleaned," she responded.

"Ammunition?"

"No," both she and Aiden said at the same time.

He looked her in the eye to gauge the truthfulness.

"My grandchild is in this house 80 percent of the time, do you think I'm crazy?" she motioned to the room. "But go ahead, search."

Lex walked out of the room. She could hear her son say something about reasonable search as the team spread out in her home. She knew they wouldn't find anything, but the thought of someone taking that gun made her angry, more than she thought it would. It was special, Lilah's last gift to her before she got sick.

She rationalized herself back into an acceptable place. It had to be that way. After all, having a registered gun that wasn't involved in a crime was supposed to be a diversion. For just this situation. Maybe not quite this situation, though. She contemplated the mistake, the huge mistake, in not using a different model, though. It might cost her in the long run.

Lex sighed, frustrated with herself and her stupid obsession with the 60DS. There were thousands of gun choices, but she just had to have that one as "the other gun." The same damn gun.

Almost four hours later, they were done. No noticeable mess. Not at all like movies. Everything was put back as close to how it was found. No mass destruction. At least there was that. Still, Lex knew she would spend the rest of the day into night rearranging every table, drawer, box, bed...they had searched Avery's little princess bed.

'*Assholes,*' she thought.

"I do have to take the gun," Detective Dixon told her, reminding himself to be professional. This was an investigation. She was a suspect. Still, she had a way about her, a look, her demeanor, that made him feel apologetic.

"I'll get it back though, right?" Lex asked.

"If it's not found to be the source of Mr. Matthews's injury," he answered.

"Please don't...don't let anything happen to it. It's important to me," she replied politely. The thought of it being destroyed was more than she could handle.

"I'm sure it will be returned in one piece," Aiden told her as they watched them leave. He looked at his watch. He was on in an hour. He wondered if he should have someone cover for him and stay with his mom. He didn't like the tone in her voice: silent politeness, it made him nervous.

Lex smiled at him.

"Go," she told him.

"Mom, I can stay, really. I don't want to leave you alone," he offered.

She hugged him.

"Go on, I'll be fine. Promise. I'm just going to rest most of the day anyway. You're bringing Avery tomorrow, right?"

"Are you sure?" Aiden asked.

"Shut up," she said, hitting his arm lightly. "What am I, five? Bring my grandchild tomorrow morning. I mean it."

"What about this weekend?" Aiden asked her cautiously. "You know, we don't have to go..."

Lex cut him off:

"Go. Seriously. I'm fine."

She watched him leave. When she was sure he wouldn't turn around and come back, she headed to Avery's room and ripped off the sheets angrily. She did the same for her bed and every other bed and began washing them.

She saw herself as a child: scrubbing her clothes to get out bloodstains, the tears running down her face, the panic of the clothes not coming clean. She could picture herself scrubbing that material together in her hands with the remnants of a piece of bar soap, running it under cold water, then warm, then cold.

As the washer ran, she wiped down every surface, re-folded clothes, and replaced the items that were touched. Her arm was still sore, and she knew this was irrational, but she was compelled to wipe away any disturbance, any trace of those people touching her stuff. It was only in fluffing the last pillow did she start to feel less manic. Only then could she breathe. Only then could she shower. She stared at herself in the mirror as the steam began to rise. It was 3 a.m.

Once clean, she curled up on the sofa, calling the dog to her side. He wagged his tail and jumped up, laying his head in her lap. She stroked his head, then clicked the "X" on the game controller.

"Are you there?" she typed.

The character sat unresponsive. She watched it until finally her eyes were too heavy and she drifted into sleep, waking to the sound of a beep.

"What can I do for you?"

The sound of the voice made Lex jump.

"I'm ready for a distraction," Lex replied, "Who's next?"

"Why the rush?" LilyQ responded.

"I just need to be busy," Lex typed.

"What is going on?" LilyQ asked her.

Lex honestly did not know how to respond, and she was too tired to make something up:

"Just...nothing. Who's next? Come on, you were eager to have me do this work for you, I'm good at it, so let's go already."

"No," LilyQ replied.

Lex stared at 'her therapist,' not expecting that answer.

"What do you mean no?" she asked.

"Tell me what is happening?" LilyQ demanded.

"I had an altercation," Lex typed hesitantly. This wasn't exactly a lie. The questioning continued:

"Are you hurt?"

"No, not at all," she lied.

"Are you in trouble?"

"It's always possible," Lex responded. "I don't think so, though. You know I'm careful."

"Yes, I do know that," LilyQ agreed, "online. But that's online."

Then the character stood silent.

"Hello?" Lex typed.

"I'm concerned," LilyQ responded.

"I'm fine, really," Lex typed.

"The last time we talked was pretty intense. I haven't heard from you in weeks, I cannot reach out to you unless you reach out to me, and now this. These people, what we do, we can't make careless mistakes. Lives depend on us, literally. Are you really being honest that you are 100%?" LilyQ asked.

Lex sighed and agreed:

"You're right."

"I think you already knew that," LilyQ stated. "So, what's up?"

"I just spent all night cleaning every inch of my home," Lex answered, "I just...I couldn't...I don't know, everything seemed so...unclean."

"Did it help?" LilyQ asked.

"No. It was like showering...the scalding hot water peeling away filth, smell, except the water was never hot enough to truly get clean," Lex explained.

"Why do you think you did that?" LilyQ commented. "What happened?"

"Everything felt dirty. I had to clean it," she responded.

"But did cleaning everything help?"

Lex thought about the question for a few seconds before responding, not quite sure she knew the answer:

"Yes? No, not really, but my house is clean." She laughed at her own response.

"Well, there's that," LilyQ stated, "I'm sorry."

"Why? You didn't do anything," Lex typed.

"Someone should have been there to help you so you didn't feel this way," LilyQ explained.

"Oh," Lex said out loud.

"Maybe the next time that happens, you could reach out first. Let's try to work through some of this. Take some time for now, though, take care of you for a while first. Is that ok? I promise there will always be something next for you to do. Unfortunately."

"Sure, yeah," Lex replied absently.

"That does not sound reassuring," LilyQ commented.

"I'm not good with idle time," Lex explained.

"Well then, I guess you should be motivated to work some of this out," LilyQ said matter-of-factly, which sounded funny coming from the avatar.

"Wow," Lex responded sarcastically.

"I care about you," LilyQ typed.

"You do not know me," Lex typed back.

"I know that you are still here. I know that you have helped me. That is worth something, right?" LilyQ stated.

"I suppose," Lex replied.

"Get some rest," LilyQ told her, "Reach out whenever you want to talk. Maybe even if you don't want to talk. Consistently. You'll know when you are ready to jump back in."

Lex closed the screen. Her eyes were hot and wet. She hadn't even realized that she was crying. It was true, though: her focus should be on cleaning up what she could to stay ahead of the detectives. It was time to take back control.

27

'In between a rock and a hard place, tryna find your way through the dark days...And everybody says they're fine, but I know we're not alright' -Papa Roach

Aiden laid awake in the hotel room staring through the dark at a crack in the ceiling. In the opposite bed, Avery turned with a small sigh, and he heard the soft bounce of a toy dropping to the floor. She was not a calm sleeper. In fact, he couldn't remember a time when she didn't end up in the opposite direction in her bed with one or more body parts hanging off, blankets on the floor, stuffed animals everywhere.

Next to him, Allison slept soundly, and he tried to focus on the quiet rhythm of her breathing, hoping it would lull him to sleep: a luxury that didn't come to him easily these days. He hated the worry he now felt and couldn't shake.

Mortality loomed over him like a dark storm cloud: his mother's...his own. Death was an occupational hazard of sorts, and he remembered the conversations about this with Lilah when he first started med school, while he was young and death seemed foreign and something that only really happened to older people, like his grandfather. It seemed so compartmentalized back then.

He had been missing Lilah a lot lately. When she died, he had Lex to turn to. When Lex got hurt, he realized just how fragile she really was, and it shook his sense of everything. For the first time, he was faced with the prospect that one day she would be gone as well, and the thought was overwhelming. He realized how lucky he was to have a parent to help guide him through life and through tragedy, even as an adult.

He missed being able to take that feeling of security for granted, a feeling that left him the moment Allison called him from the emergency room, luckily rounding, when Lex was brought in:

"Babe, you need to get down here...it's your mom."

Allison's panicked voice saying those words still echoed in his head.

Lex had seemed small to him in the hospital bed and for the first time, mortal. Suddenly he'd realized that he didn't really know her as a person. She was just 'Mom,' like her existence began when he became a sentient being. Even Lilah had history: Grandpa Al's life, his home, stories of Emily, his wife, and stories of Lilah as a child, these were all part of his history. Lex was always just a part of that history and not her own. He remembered asking where 'mommy's' mom and dad were, and he remembered the answer to be something like, "Sometimes people don't have a mom and dad," and he remembered just accepting that answer.

It occurred to him now that his parents were very sly as he thought about times when he brought that up and how easily they deflected this with something else and he, being a kid or a teenager, and being self-focused, always ran with it.

That his parents had secrets that they purposely kept from him, especially Lilah, the open book that she was, made him question their life. And his life. Lex could have died and with that, whole pieces of her, of them that he never knew, and though he understood completely that people have their own lives, private lives, this was a big one. Lex as someone else, someone unrecognizable, was a big one. Almost losing her made him think about Avery losing him one day. Would he have secrets that she would never know? What if he died without her really knowing him? Would he die without really knowing his mom?

These thoughts plagued him often now. It wasn't rational, it was existential. He wanted to understand why he had so much doubt now. He wanted to understand why he didn't believe his mom about the accident. He was beginning to doubt her intentions with everything: going to Hawaii with a minute's notice, and a sudden interest in Avery attending preschool. In the deepest, darkest corner of his being, he thought just a little that maybe his mom knew more about the man who almost killed her. He needed to know the real Lex so that he could talk himself out of the crazy notion that maybe his mother did shoot the man.

At the same moment while Aiden lay awake in that Chicago hotel room trying to figure out who his mother really was, Lex worked to erase the part of who she was that she never wanted him, or anyone, to know. She clicked the 'X' on the game controller. Her wrist ached holding it in place.

'New Game?' appeared on the screen. Lex highlighted 'Yes' and clicked the 'X' again. She chose 'New Task.' 'Choose Characters' appeared next. She chose the little blonde girl, the character created for Avery, and a school backpack as her item. 'Adversary?' She chose 'No,' ignoring the various figures that had been modified and painted by her granddaughter. It made her smile, looking at the stick figure blobs of color with drawn on smiles.

Making 'Mr. Staley' completely disappear 'phase two' was a challenge. Sure, she had taken care of the basics, the things that any detective would look into. The things that would have been enough had she not been so closely attached via the accident. There was so much unknown: Did anyone know he came out here? That he was looking for his sister? Was there physical evidence where he lived that could lead anyone to her? Those were details she could do nothing about, probably ever.

Instead, Lex began to focus a more extensive search on what she could control. Methodically, the little girl made her way through the maze:

North Branch Correctional Institution – Jacob Staley. Rape, Assault. Paroled. The little character retrieved a pencil from the backpack and erased the link connecting this fact to any external search engine. Next, Prince George's County Circuit Court: Lexus link erased and the file, though accessible locally, hidden to the world. Piece by piece, the little girl made her way through Maryland databases. Did Lex need to use the facade of the game to do this? No. But the little character made the seriousness of the situation bearable. What Lex wanted, though, the holy grail of identification: a birth certificate, was nowhere to be found. She found Melissa's easily, but obviously, her brother wasn't born in the same place, or with the same name.

Systematically, everything else was hidden or removed. DMV, gone, Social Security, gone. The little girl put these 'documents' into her backpack, brought them back to home base, emptied the backpack into a bin and set them on fire. Lex watched this play out on the screen as the dog's insistent whine told Lex that it was now morning.

"Okay already...let's get you a treat," she told him.

Lex stood and stretched. The hours glued to one spot had taken a toll; her eyes were dry, her body ached, reminding her that she definitely no longer had the stamina of a 20-year-old. Regardless, she had no way of knowing what Detective Dixon had already discovered. Sleep would have to wait; it was time to ensure Mr. Matthews had more dimension. How Jacob had gotten that identity she couldn't know, but having it was an advantage he had unwittingly given her. And lucky for her, his wallet was found at the scene. It delayed the forensic identification, though Lex was sure that was in process.

"Thank you, Eric Matthews," Lex said out loud as she retrieved a gem from a treasure chest and placed it into a case. It would have been so easy to make him disappear as well, make him a complete no one. She gave Detective Dixon some credit. He and his partner seemed like the type to enjoy the chase. Confirming his identity would make the chase less interesting. The gem connected the fingerprints to the man on the driver's license.

By late afternoon, Eric Matthews had a complete history. A drifter. Odd jobs. In and out of jail for petty theft, narcotics. Grew up in Yuma Arizona. Nothing significant. Temporary resident of a low rent hotel. Prints a match to a string of burglaries over the last few months and to a bundle of cocaine seized at the border. Perhaps this would lead them to another theory, that whomever shot him had something to do with narcotics. Lex hoped it was just enough for the detectives to exhaust their search and let her life return to normal.

She made her way to her bedroom and laid across her bed. Her eyes focused on the empty gun case. Lex knew she would have to retrieve the gun. The real gun. For a moment, she thought about asking for advice. There had to be others doing for LilyQ what she had been asked to do who were discreet and non-existent like she was. She thought of all places to be honest, for someone to truly understand the circumstances, and not judge, this would be the place. But almost everything she had shared... they were the memories of a victim, of someone who had experienced the darkness that people were capable of. This was completely different. Talking to this nameless, hidden person helped her feel calm, but not calm enough to ask for that type of help. A secret was only truly a secret if only you knew what it was.

'No,' she thought, 'you don't really know. There are some real psychos out there.'

Lex laughed at the irony. The gun would have to wait for a while.

"Hey," she asked the dog, "want to go to the park and see some friends tomorrow?"

'...everyone says they're fine, but I know we're not alright.'

28

"What do you mean it isn't a match?" Erin Hereford asked in disbelief. "That doesn't make any sense."

Even with the rush job, unlike the movies, it took a few weeks to get the ballistics results back. This annoyed Erin more than anything.

"It isn't a match," Marcus repeated, "the gun we tested did not shoot Eric Matthews."

"Anything from the hotel room?" Detective Dixon inquired, trying to ignore his partner's agitation.

"Tons of prints. Honestly, it's taking a while to process them, but so far what has come back doesn't match Alexis Vance or anyone in her family," Marcus answered, adding: "You were right about the ashes...they were pictures. Beyond recovery. Oh, and he paid for everything in cash."

"His prints? DNA? Anything?" the young woman demanded in frustration.

"Yes. Tons from the recovered body. Eric Matthews. Some minor crimes. Drugs. Moved around a lot. Looks like he was responsible for a couple burglaries. Also attached to some impounded drugs in San Diego. No social media."

Detective Hereford gave Marcus 'the look.'"Right," he said, "I'll let you know when I have more. But right now, honestly, there is nothing to tie Alexis Vance to anything other than the car accident."

"Damn it!" Detective Hereford exclaimed angrily, "I thought this was going to tie them together."

"Well, a man was shot and then attempted to run down someone randomly. That's a pretty interesting coincidence, right?" Marcus asked.

Detective Dixon sighed as he listened to their back and forth.

"Not really," he interrupted finally, "no evidence, no case."

He already guessed this would be the outcome and had tried to prepare his young partner to expect the same. Still, she had been convinced that this would be easy. He thought she must have watched way too much *CSI* or *Law and Order* growing up.

He turned to leave. "Erin, you coming?"

She turned towards him hesitantly.

"Good work," he told her. "Don't obsess about this case. Or any case, for that matter. You won't be able to sleep at night. Put it to bed."

"Ok, I'll be up in a minute," she told him.

"Maybe the additional prints will give us a new lead at some point," he commented on his way out of the lab, "Meanwhile, move on."

She nodded and waited for Detective Dixon to walk out of earshot before turning back to the lab tech.

"Anything yet?" she inquired.

"The OnStar? No," Marcus told her. "She goes to the dog park in the morning, sometimes she's there for a couple hours, sometimes all day, sometimes she stays home. She goes to the preschool to pick up her granddaughter, to the store, to her son's place. It's all pretty regular."

"And at the park?"

"Well, the dog is running back and forth and in circles, but I don't imagine she is. Honestly, it seems like a normal routine. I don't have more. It was a good thought, tracking the dog's GPS, though," Marcus replied.

"But all day?" the detective continued, ignoring his comment.

"I'm not a spy, Hereford. I mean, there's dog training, hiking, tai chi, chess? Do people still sit and read in the park these days? Who knows? What I know is what the technology reports," he answered honestly, adding, "didn't Dix just say to put it to bed?"

Erin tapped her fingers on the table. "He said for me to move on, and I am. Let me know if something changes," she commanded.

"Like what? A trip to the mall or post office? Spending New Years' Eve at Olive Garden?" Marcus said sarcastically, adding, "How long are you going to chase the dragon?"

"As long as it takes," Detective Hereford told him. Sure, she was new to this, but not new to her gut, and it told her that Alexis Vance was hiding something, and she was going to figure out what it was, even if it took a while.

29

"I'm not a perfect person...there's many things I wish I didn't do..." -Hoobastank

A light breeze swept across the blue of late May catching the back of Lex's neck, cooling her slightly as it grazed her sun warmed skin. In the repetition of activity, she had lost herself in thought. It was everything, it was nothing. It was the calm silence of focus and the hiss of helium as she filled balloons. It was the quiet sound of Avery humming to herself and the splash of the pool water as she pretended to make her dolls swim.

"Gramma, why are we having a party for my baby sister if she isn't born yet?" Avery asked from the pool's baja.

Lex tied off a balloon she had just filled with helium.

"Well, we want her to be born, right? So, if we have a party for her with cake and presents, maybe she will want to hurry up," she answered.

Even though Avery was aware on the calendar that her baby sister would be born in July, she still asked at least once a week when her sister would be born.

"We should have had a party already then. I've been waiting too long," the child commented absently.

"Good point," Lex responded, amused at her perspective. "The thing is, she still had to grow all her parts, and now that she has, we need to let her know to be born."

"Oh. Makes sense," Avery responded.

Lex laughed. Avery had been saying that a lot lately.

"Why is it called a baby shower?" Avery asked her.

"You know, I have no idea," Lex answered honestly, remembering her own when she was pregnant with Aiden:

"Why do we have to have a baby shower?" she had asked Lilah.

"Because that's what people do when they have a baby," Lilah replied. "Honestly, Lex, why are you so resistant? Everyone wants to celebrate this with us."

'Not everyone,' she'd thought, 'I haven't confirmed.'

It had really been for Lilah anyway as most 'intimate, relational' events were. Being at the center of everyone's attention was not Lex's idea of a good time and made her uncomfortable. She preferred going out just the two of them, mingling with strangers.

A lifetime ago, Lex had enjoyed the way Lilah liked to show her off, like she was something won, and she enjoyed showing up to events dressed in some sexy outfit, hair and make-up perfected, the real enjoyment captured in those first moments...in the look on Lilah's face and the way she responded when Lex walked into a room. She found herself missing that.

"Lilah would have loved this," she said quietly to herself as she filled another balloon.

In the months following the 'accident,' Lex worked to settle into a life less complicated. Which was exhausting. Things appeared calm; the police weren't at her doorstep to arrest her anyway, but the threat still loomed. Staying ahead of an investigation or any possible lead was complicated, especially since she had no real insight into what was being investigated. Keeping a routine, one that didn't seem practiced or perfect, was a difficult challenge: consistent interaction with people as she studied the routine in others...stop and chat with Mr. Morrison about his upcoming surgery, talk to dog owners randomly about dog food or training, make sure her voice was heard playing with the dog, hiking various trails, wearing clothes that were indistinguishable from other women.

This facade was a thoughtful and carefully executed diversion for a life more suited to her: the normal ebb and flow of tasks, either solicited or 'assigned,' the cautious interaction with LilyQ, whose promised 'progress' that was supposed to stop the nightmares and anxiety seemed painfully slow. And, as LilyQ often stated, it was only as good as the truth she shared. So really slow.

Lex was aware that she was under moderate surveillance; her OnStar being tracked, an unmarked vehicle occasionally parked down the street. This wasn't Dixon, she was sure of that. This was the young detective, and she had been easy to read. Erin Hereford was determined, a young woman finding her place and trying to stand out in a world where it was hard to stand out. Lex would have admired that if it wasn't directed at her.

Detective Hereford was tech savvy, well, Marcus Jackson was, and she knew how to make use of the many tools at her disposal. Lex thought about how nice it was back when computer technology was still foreign to most. Now children were coding, and every law enforcement agency had a specialist. Granted, most had learned the "how to" from a classroom and very few had any natural talent.

That they must think that she was naive bothered Lex. True, this let her fly under the radar in spite of herself and really allowed her room to breathe and keep the anxiety minimal, but still, it was annoying. She was supposed to be naive, careless. That was the reason for the routine: create a good offense, let time go by. Let them think she was oblivious, ignore the fact that they were tracking her vehicle, ignore that they were tracking her dog. Be normal, boring. Bored.

She wished she wasn't a godless child. Maybe then she would have that "something" built in that would stop her from so much of what she had done, that something that should have made her feel remorse for killing Melissa, who was herself a godless child, and considering what she came from, maybe deserving of some mercy and understanding...just not hers.

Lex wasn't devoid of feeling: she loved Lilah, she was sure of that. She loved her son, and Avery, and even Allison. It was just different now, not something safe but something that could be lost and in need of protection. LilyQ had asked her about that: did she love someone? What was her relationship like with her child? She admitted that she wasn't as close as she would like.

"Why do you think that is?" LilyQ had asked.

"I don't know," Lex had responded at first.

"What do you think your child would think about what you do, about what we have been doing?" she continued.

"I don't know, this is separate from that," Lex stated.

"Do you think that this keeps you from having a closer relationship?" LilyQ asked.

"Are you trying to lose me as a resource?" Lex replied sarcastically, avoiding the question.

LilyQ laughed as she responded:

"No, not at all. It's something to think about, though. I'm confident that it isn't the only factor. I guess a better question is: Do you want to be closer?"

"To my kid?" Lex asked.

"To anyone," LilyQ responded.

'Only Lilah,' Lex thought without answering, wondering if Lilah would have forgiven her for all of this, for all she never knew, and wishing for the first time in ages that there was a heaven for her, a faith that could justify and forgive who she was. Or at least provide a safety net to quiet the feeling of being alone that existed as its own entity occupying space in her soul.

Never had there been a time when Lex had been free from this. Even in the happiest times of her life, this 'alone' sat ready to take over. This was something to run from, to lie to and bargain with so as not to be swallowed by it.

Lilah had been great at seeing it...even if she couldn't destroy it...even in the younger days of their relationship when Lex was struggling, having been left without someone who truly lived it. Without Cody, who in spite of everything, understood this type of "alone," and there was a certain emptiness that she couldn't calm.

It had been raining hard the day when Lilah first asked about it. The large drops pelted against the bedroom window, seeping slightly through the screen. They laid in bed listening to the downpour, and Lilah, noticing the water, got up to close the window.

"Leave it," Lex told her.

"It's raining in," Lilah responded.

"Leave it, I want to hear it," she reiterated.

Lilah, undeterred, closed the window anyway.

"You can still hear it," she told her as she shut it.

"Not as loudly," Lex replied, reaching for and turning on the radio.

As music quietly resonated from the small device, Lilah got back into bed. She started to speak, then stopped herself.

"What?" Lex asked.

"Nothing," she answered, "Never mind."

"No, what were you going to say?" Lex insisted.

Lilah rolled onto her side, propping her head in her hand.

Lex could picture her perfectly, her hair down and messy from sleep, the blanket pulled around her barely covering her body: a picture of perfection.

"You don't like the quiet, do you?" she asked.

"What do you mean?" Lex responded.

"Well...other than truly sleeping and moments coming and going, there is always sound: the TV, the radio, headphones. It is never quiet here.

"The silence is too loud," Lex offered, sighing.

"What does that even mean?" Lilah asked, reaching out to brush her fingers through Lex's hair.

"I don't know, it's too loud; it kind of takes over, makes my brain feel confused and dark, you know?"

Lilah shook her head no as Lex added:

"It's like there's something inside, like something dark living inside...fear, isolation, that I can't get away from. It feels bigger when it's quiet."

"Is it like keeping a secret, like something you need to talk about?" Lilah asked softly.

"No," Lex replied, "it's like a voice...not a voice..."

"A feeling? Like depressed or sad?" Lilah interrupted.

"No. Not really. It's like...another me. Or something. It makes me feel separate."

"From me?" Lilah asked.

"From everything," Lex responded quickly. "It makes me feel hollow. Empty."

"Oh," Lilah responded.

Lex knew she didn't understand. All the people Lex knew...no one did. Except Cody.

"You don't get it," Lex stated.

Lilah smiled softly, moving closer.

"Nope," she said quietly as she pulled Lex to her, kissing her softly on the neck, "Silence is overrated anyway."

Lilah had a way, without understanding, of making Lex feel understood. If there was a Heaven, Lilah would surely be there. If there was Heaven, Lex was surely going to Hell. It was better not to think about it, better to kill the past, better to focus on the present, on blowing up balloons, on watching Avery splash around in the pool.

Aiden hadn't made that very easy, first with the hovering, often wondering out loud why the police were waiting so long to return her stuff, the odds of all of this happening. Then an abrupt switch to an interest in her past, asking about her childhood, her parents, where she grew up...

"Why the sudden interest in all of this irrelevant information?" she had asked, to which he replied something about wanting to know her, about the new baby and Avery having family history.

Finding new things to tell him that were true but unrelated to the mess that her life was before Lilah was challenging and, admittedly, also a bit annoying. What was Lex supposed to say? That she spent most of her early years in chaos? That she got lucky and discovered a gift for programming and erased herself? That Lex really wasn't Lex? Lilah had always accepted her boundaries, but unlike Lilah, her son was relentless...

...so was Detective Hereford with her constant surveillance; another one keeping Lex from completely moving forward. How many times had she shopped at that Food 4 Less without giving into the temptation to even quickly glance over to the spot where she and Jacob had their one and only confrontation? Though surely rain had long ago washed away any blood, one glance and anyone who might be following her would surely search for, and discover, the gun. Hence the normal boring routine.

The baby shower was a clear reminder of the weight hanging over her head. Lex again cursed Erin Hereford's persistence. The weight of unfinished business hung over her like the ominous thunderheads hanging heavy over the mountains in the distance, and Lex felt even more distracted than usual, the laughter and happy anticipation surrounding her overshadowed by this last loose end. She had waited, week after week, unsure of herself, doubting that she had worked through every possible scenario.

But it was almost summer now. Soon it would be too hot for the park and then what? Wait until Autumn? The growing panic would be unbearable by then. This was the time: The events were right, the predicted weather optimal...she hadn't been physically followed in weeks...

It was a good plan, and yet, in spite of the long exhausting day of setting up for the party, entertaining and cleaning up, Lex laid awake most of the night second guessing everything. She hadn't felt this uncertain since the confrontation.

'At least you still feel something,' she thought, absently twisting her rings around her finger.

30

"Good morning, Ana," Lex said with a smile as she took a parking pass at the park entrance.

"Good morning, Miss Lex," the attendant replied, "gonna be a hot one."

"Looks like it," Lex responded. "Have a good day."

Lex pulled around past the first lot, winding through the park to the backlot, closer to the hiking trails, to a line of cars mostly indistinguishable from any other. She backed into a spot, just like Carole Stewart, whose grey SUV was a few spots down. Carole would be at a booth in the farmer's market, selling honey from her own bee farm. Sundays 8 a.m. to 3 p.m.

Lex leashed the dog and made her way down a short path to the picnic area where several groups of people were setting up for various parties with streamers, balloons, banners.

She walked over to a man standing on a bench hanging a piñata over a tree branch: The General, as he was known, due to the faded Army cap and his passion for telling stories of his military adventures. When he had formally introduced himself, she remembered thinking that his name was almost irrelevant, an afterthought. His true personality, everything about him, was the General.

"Good morning, General," she said, loud enough for him to hear, but not too loud for fear she'd startle him.

"Lex," he acknowledged, not looking back or pausing from his activity. Of course, he knew she was behind him, his sense of awareness sharp from experience.

"For Christina," she said, setting a gift down on a bench.

His dog, Clide, upon hearing her voice, wagged his tail and barked. Lex bent down to pet him.

"Where's your grandbaby? Need any help setting up?" she asked the General, anticipating the answer.

Nodding in the direction of a man and woman carrying party supplies, he responded, "Got it under control. Hiking?"

"Yes sir. I want to get in a good one before it gets too hot," she replied, turning back to Clide. "How 'bout a treat, buddy?"

Both dogs wagged their tails as she reached into her small backpack, feeling around for treats, stopping her hand first on a small remote, which she clicked, before removing her hand with treats for both dogs.

"See you later, then," she commented as she walked away.

"Cake later," he called after her.

"Got it," she replied.

Lex always respected his responses, direct and short, more like orders than conversation. No emotion, no 'tell.' Honest. He only truly came alive telling stories of his past or talking about his granddaughter.

She walked briskly on a path through the more populated park landscape, saying hi to several of the regulars prior to winding up a hiking trail, then backtracked through the brush to her vehicle. She strapped the dog in quietly then pulled out, stopping her vehicle in front of Carole's. She pulled out her phone and entered a code, disrupting her OnStar signal and tethering it to the parked vehicle. The signal would take twenty to thirty seconds to make the change, a detail that could not be changed or controlled. It felt like an eternity.

Finally, a signal beeped success. The dog tracker, though, she could only hope that the signal actually tethered her dog to Clide: something she couldn't know until later and truly a long shot as far as an alibi. It was almost location specific. If it came down to detail, she was supposed to be hiking, and Clide was running around in the park.

These fine little details were what kept Lex awake at night, running through every possible scenario that might lead her to fail. Regardless, she was in motion now. She drove up an old service road, watching for any witnesses. As she expected, there were none; this was too far off any hiking path or park activity.

Once out of the park, she sighed in relief as she sped towards the freeway, looking at her watch. The General had excitedly discussed the schedule of his granddaughter's party activities, and he was extremely punctual, probably no match for the erratic behavior of a bunch of six year olds, but nonetheless, on a schedule. A hike around Carter Canyon was around five hours. She had approximately five and a half hours until cake.

First stop, the wash close to Food 4 Less. Lex climbed up the side of it and down into the grown over field, hoping that it would keep her somewhat hidden. There was no other way to reach the storm drain unless she actually parked in the parking lot, of course, not an option in daylight. She crouched to almost a crawl as she eased closer to the drain. Spring had at least given her the gift of overgrown, wild landscape, which, if she kept low, might just hide her enough from the shoppers in the parking lot since it was blistering hot and shoppers would most likely park as close to the entrance as possible.

The sun beamed hot and uncomfortable, and her thighs burned from crouching.

"I'm too fucking old for this," she muttered under her breath as she pulled up the cover and reached into the wet, muddy sludge, fumbling her hand around. The feeling of slime, even through her gloved hand, caused her to shiver.

Lex pulled up the plastic bag, confirming it was what she came for, then felt around in the slime to ensure the gloves she'd left behind had washed away, and not finding them, she crawled away, running as soon as she could, almost tripping over her own feet.

The dog, left in the car, was barking wildly, not at all happy to be left behind.

"Alright, enough!" she scolded quietly as she started the vehicle and sped towards the freeway. She checked her watch. Four hours and forty-five minutes left: this had taken twenty minutes longer than she estimated. She sped east, towards Palm Springs, watching ahead as the clouds gathered over the mountains in the distance.

31

"So, I walk upon high and step to the edge to see my world below" –Collective Soul

The desert rains fell in the distance....working, pounding, reshaping the baked red clay. More often than not, it was cool and wet in one place and warm and dry in another.

Lex always liked the desert. When she was especially haunted and needed to find peace, she imagined herself in its openness during the summer monsoons. She'd stand in the middle of miles from nowhere as the sun's intensity stood in stillness at a dry 110 degrees. The sky above would be blinding yellow, just vaguely tinted powder blue.

This was where Lex found herself. The path to the storm drain had been a challenge; relationships, hiking, waiting...but there she stood with the gun. Finally.

She looked out across the vast miles of nowhere to the place where the skies were a dark, threatening shield of gray and black, brilliant as the sun sent its bright sword rays to do battle for control of the afternoon sky.

She watched the rain pouring over the earth, moving closer and closer to her in a great sheet. She had counted on the consistent nature of the monsoons.

She closed her eyes.

The stillness and silence of the intense heat pulsated like an invisible, living second skin around her body.

She waited.

First, there was the scent: sweet of wet earth.

Next came the breeze: barely cool but just slight enough to cause a chill.

The sound followed: the large, fast drops slapping the baked, bleached-red earth.

Suddenly, she found herself at the center of the storm. Just as the drops pounded and worked their way into the earth, she felt them pound and work their way through the second heat skin, then through her body. She felt as though there was no separation between herself and the rain. She felt the drops pouring over her body, over her eyes and down her face where many years of tears should have poured.

Instead, there was the rain; to replenish the earth...to relieve the cracking frame...to cry sweetly.

Then just as suddenly, the storm moved on. The sun returned and with it, eerie calm.

Lex took apart the gun and, piece by piece, tossed it into the impromptu streams, watching each piece as it washed away in different directions in the rushing water.

She sighed deeply. It was always for her, the sun, as it began to warm her skin that caused the chill in her spine. But...while in the storm, for another moment, she was held, protected and peaceful.

True peace, though, was short lived: Time was passing quickly. Two hours. She had to get back.

When she reached Ontario, Lex pulled into a TA truck stop. In the bathroom, she changed from wet clothes to dry then tossed the gloves in the bathroom wastebasket and the wet clothes into one of the already running washing machines. She washed down the car mat and her seats with paper towels and hosed down her tires and the underbelly of her vehicle. Lastly, she hosed down her muddy shoes and socks and tossed them into a bin.

Once back at the park, she held her breath as she pulled back down into the backlot, sighing with relief when she spotted Carole's SUV still parked. She pulled in front of it and just as she did earlier, typed code into her phone, untethering the vehicles, then she parked, not in the same spot, but close enough.

She ran the dog up a short trail, enough to sweat, enough to make the dog pant, then made her way back to the main park. It was busier now, kids running around everywhere, the smell of BBQ in the air...and the General's cake still intact. She walked up to him.

"Having fun?" she asked him, still out of breath.

"Running behind," he answered matter-of-factly, smiling at his granddaughter. He looked at his watch.

"Carter Canyon?" He said, more as a comment then a question.

"Yes," Lex replied with a tired smile.

"Made good time," he said. "Trail good today?"

He motioned for her to sit down, which she did gratefully, and she replied:

"Long. A little warmer than I anticipated. Quiet."

"Good deal. Have you seen Carole today?" he replied.

Lex smiled, pulling out the collapsible dog bowl, clicking the dog remote. The General had a slight crush on the Bee farmer.

"Saw her SUV," she said slyly.

The General gave her a stern look but commented politely, "I should bring her a piece of cake."

As Lex raised a water bottle to her lips, she noticed that her hand was shaking. So did the General.

"You should eat something," he told her.

She nodded in agreement.

32

Erin Hereford raced steadily uphill on her stationary bike, music in one ear, MSNBC silent on the screen in front of her. She glanced intermittently at the stats, keeping pace as the time counted down: Five, four, three, two...the program beeped success. She checked her pulse before hopping off the bike. It was higher than normal, a side effect from both neglecting exercise on a regular basis and the poor eating habits of a detective's schedule.

Showering, she made a mental note to re-dedicate to a healthier lifestyle. On the counter, her phone buzzed, and she ignored it, opting to close her eyes and let the water run over her neck and shoulders. She knew it was work, it was always work, and she would be there soon enough. The buzzing stopped, and a few seconds later, the phone beeped with a text message.

She sighed and reached through the shower door to read it.

"Call me." It was from Marcus.

"Fuck," she said out loud, simultaneously redialing, turning off the water and grabbing a towel.

"What's up, Marcus?" she asked.

"I'm great, how are you?" he said.

"Hello, Marcus, how are you today?" she said, rolling her eyes.

"I'm having a great day..." he began.

"Ok, Marcus, really, I'm on in an hour. What's up?" she interrupted.

"Well, it's about Alexis Vance. You asked for changes, anomalies...

Erin's heart raced. Less than forty-five minutes later, she found Marcus at his desk.

"Show me," she commanded, pulling over a chair.

"As I said on the phone, it might be nothing," he commented.

Her silence told him to continue.

"Ok, see? Here," he said pointing to a grid, "I noticed it when I got in today."

"What exactly am I looking at?" she asked.

"So, there was an interruption of service," he told her.

"Is OnStar even on when you park?" she asked.

"That's not the point," he continued, "So, she was parked, see right here. Then just twenty minutes later, the car moved, which on its own is off pattern, but, right here...the signal is gone."

"Gone like, off?" she asked.

"No, gone like poof, it was there, then gone, then back in the same place about thirty seconds later and no more movement," he explained.

"What do you think it is? An anomaly?" Erin asked.

"If it was one time...I could see that...but twice? In the same spot?" He moved the grid to another point before continuing, "This just happened fifteen minutes ago."

"What are you thinking?" Erin asked him then.

"I don't know exactly. The signal was definitely interrupted," Marcus replied, turning to face Erin, "You asked me to keep you apprised of inconsistencies. There have been two in a five-hour gap. I don't think it's a coincidence. Since I don't know what happened, I can't guarantee that the vehicle is even there. And before you ask, the dog, at least its signal, has been, and still is, in the park."

"Damn it!" Erin exclaimed, heading for the door.

"What are you going to do? It might be nothing," Marcus called after her.

"Oh, it's something," she shot back at him. "I'm going to send patrol out to see if the vehicle is there."

"And then what?" he asked. "Like I said, you can't arrest someone for a satellite glitch."

"If she's not there, then I have good reason to bring her in. I think we got her," Erin told him.

"That's a pretty big stretch," he called out as the elevator doors closed.

"Why do I bother?" he said under his breath, turning back to his screen.

33

Lex watched the General and Carole converse. Though she couldn't hear the conversation, it appeared light and pleasant. She wondered if they would eventually get together. It would have been nice to see that through, but this whole long scenario was all for one purpose: to bide time and create the perfect alibi to dispose of the gun. And that task was now completed.

She looked down at her watch: 3 p.m.

'Time to go,' she thought, standing.

She caught the General's eye and waved to him as she left. He nodded and went back to his conversation, and she wondered how much longer she really needed to come to the park.

She could not abruptly change her routine; obviously, that would have to continue for a few more weeks, until it made sense that it was reasonably too hot to hike. Lex thought about this as she drove through the lot. That would carry her through summer, and by then Allison would probably be back to work, and she would have her new granddaughter to care for. And maybe at summer's end, she would bring the baby a couple times into early autumn. But after? Maybe it would make sense to keep these relationships 'just in case'.

Lex paid the parking fee and exited the park. She was on autopilot, realizing just how draining this had been. Her mind drifted to Allison, so worried and excited at having a baby. She silently promised to give her the support that Lilah had once given her. Her thought was short lived as the siren behind her brought her sharply back to reality.

"Oh, fuck," Lex said out loud.

What had she missed?

She caught her breath as the officer approached her door. She could see in the mirror that his hand was cautiously resting on his gun.

She rolled down the window.

"Was I speeding?" she said calmly.

"Step out of the car, please," he ordered.

Lex sighed, thinking to herself, *'Here we go...'*

"What about my dog?" she said as the officer handcuffed her.

He was barking uncontrollably, and the officer seemed a bit unsure of himself.

"Can I call my son? He's only about ten minutes from here. Please. Just let him come get the dog," she pleaded.

The officer held the cellphone to her ear.

"Aiden. Listen, to me. Don't panic. They're taking me in for questioning," she told him calmly.

"What!" Aiden shouted through the phone.

"Listen! I don't exactly know what is going on. I'm by the park, I'm in handcuffs. Just come get the dog," she said quietly.

"What the fuck?" he questioned. "That's it. I'm getting an attorney. Don't say anything."

By then, another officer had arrived.

"Well, I don't have anything to say," she told him. "Find the General. At the park, there's a birthday party. He'll tell you. I just came from a hike," Lex moved her ear away from the phone, telling the officer, "My son wants to talk to you..." as the other officer 'helped' her into the car.

34

'Well, no one told me about her, the way she lied'
-The Zombies

Lex sat in a small conference room alone. She hadn't
been processed or put in a jail cell, which was at
least encouraging. And she was no longer handcuffed,
though there was an officer outside the door.

'At least Aiden got the dog,' she thought.

As time passed slowly, she went over every motion,
every step to figure out exactly where she messed up.
Was it the dog tracker? Did someone see her leaving or
entering the park on that back road? What was it? She
sat in silence.

Her poor son. What was taking so long? She let her
mind wander. Maybe they put everything together. Maybe they were telling him right now...she sucked down the
panic, resigned. This was one of the possibilities.

The door opened, and Detective Hereford entered the
room. She was quiet, but looked smug, sure of herself.

"Well," she began, "I think you know why you're here."

'Don't let her bait you,' Lex thought, saying nothing. She
read the detective's face and instantly took control. 'She's
trying to call your bluff.'

"Do yourself a favor. It's better all around if you just tell me what happened," the Detective added.

Lex looked her straight in the eyes.

"I don't know what you are talking about," she said calmly, detached. "I don't have to talk to you."

Erin's voice was soft and pleasant as she continued:

"Don't you want this to end? Aren't you tired of this?"

"What is it exactly that I am supposed to be tired of?" Lex responded just as quiet.

"Come on, really, where is the gun? Stop playing games."

Lex leaned in and whispered:

"You're really determined. I admire that in a person."

She leaned back.

"If I'm arrested, then put me in a cell, if not then I would like to leave, please," she said louder.

They stared at each other: a silent defiant battle for control of the situation. Finally, the detective looked away and stood.

"Fine," she said abruptly and left the room.

Lex sighed, relieved.

'They have nothing. So why am I here?'

Another hour passed before the door opened again: Lucas.

Now an attorney, he was once just an awkward, towheaded boy that her son grew up with.

"Luke!" she cried out in relief.

He bent over to hug her, whispering:

"Mom, Aiden's right outside. He is so pissed."

Detective Dixon walked in behind him. Lex ignored his entrance, saying instead:

"I'm not sure what is happening."

Which was technically true.

She pulled the parking pass out of her pocket and handed it to Lucas.

"See," she told him, "the park. All day."

"My apologies," Detective Dixon offered. "There was a... misunderstanding."

She was about to respond when Lucas put his hand on her shoulder.

"A satellite glitch. That's your misunderstanding?"

He continued without an answer, pulling a folded paper out of his jacket pocket.

"You pulled over my client, handcuffed her without cause and have held her in this room for hours. Then I hear that the officer was sent to confirm that my client's vehicle was in a parking lot, and I strongly question the validity of even tracking my client in the first place, however, that aside, this officer made a decision to pull her over. And then bring her in? For questioning. In handcuffs. And I have not been given a valid reason for that, if you would like to provide one."

Detective Dixon was calm, professional in his response:

"As I stated. This was a misunderstanding. We are looking into the matter and the breakdown in communication."

"You've been following me for months," Lex stated.

"Really?" Lucas commented.

"I didn't say anything because I thought it stopped. I didn't want to worry Aiden," she added.

"We're leaving," Lucas demanded, putting out his hand to help her up while saying to the detective:

"No probable cause for her to be here. False imprisonment. I've opened an inquiry into this surveillance, and we will be adding harassment to the complaint. This is egregious behavior," he told the detective.

Lex almost laughed at the statement...she had taught him that word when he was twelve.

"And I want her belongings returned," he added.

"I can assure you that this will not happen again," Detective Dixon told her. "My apologies."

Lex looked at the detective, shaking her head in acceptance.

He watched them leave, hearing her say only:

"Is my dog okay?"

He sighed heavily, swallowing the anger he felt building towards his young partner. She would be back at her desk by now, figuring the lieutenant already gave her an earful. Still, he had a lot to say.

"I didn't tell them to follow her..."

"Today," he said, cutting her off as he approached her.

"I certainly didn't say to arrest her," Erin added.

"You're done," Detective Dixon lectured. "No more tracking this woman. Even if you caught something at this point, can you really justify how you came across the data? Tracking her car with no warrant? Tracking a dog chip? Pulling resources into something by leading them to believe it was authorized? Are you serious? You need these people, and you're already burning your bridges."

"Can you really say that she is innocent?" the young detective countered. "She isn't innocent..."

"She is as far as you are concerned," he interrupted.

"Stan, come on," Erin said, throwing up her hands.

"Erin, listen," he explained calmly, "this investigation is now closed..."

Detective Hereford started to protest. He held up his hand to silence her.

"...for now," he continued. "I'm not disputing your intention. I'm not disputing that you might be right. But in my experience, which you should take advantage of, if someone is guilty of something, at some point, it will come back around. Right now...we don't need a lawsuit. Seriously, let it rest before you end your career before it even begins."

'Lucky for me, it won't be my problem,' he thought as he continued:

"I'm returning her belongings. Trust me, you have more important cases to deal with. Solvable cases. For now."

Detective Dixon took inventory of the items removed from the Vance home, checking the list and verifying that everything was accounted for and ready to be returned.

He would wait a few days to return them, one because he wanted to give time for everyone to calm down. Two because no one was going to force him to 'immediately' do anything.

Honestly, though, he wanted this off his plate. He felt for Detective Hereford. It was extremely frustrating to walk away from something that you know you are right about. What she was lacking was the insight into the actions of suspects, that until you walk away, the guard is always up. His phone beeped. A text from Marcus: "Check your email. This popped up a few days ago."

He pulled up the message and opened the report: A DNA match to Alexis Vance in the National Database. Not her DNA...a relative. He read on, and when he finished, he shook his head.

"Jesus."

He sent a text to Marcus:

"Keep this confidential."

He knew Marcus would; Erin had almost gotten him fired for his participation in her surveillance activity, and he wanted nothing to do with her right now.

He deleted the email and walked out with the box of belongings.

"Two years, five months...let it go," he told himself.

35

The morning sun peeked through the curtains of the living room. Lex was curled up on her sofa with the keyboard in her lap. Outside, the dog barked and ran back and forth as a set of birds stared down at him from a telephone wire.

"I had a nightmare," she typed.

"Tell me," her avatar therapist said.

"I am in my mom's room sitting on her bed. It is dark but the door is open, and the hall light is bright enough to light the room. I am a kid still, but old enough to babysit. It is night and my mom is at work. I can hear my sister... and my brother.

'Did I tell her I had a brother?' Lex thought.

She continued:

"I think they are in my brother's room. I walk out into the hallway. My intention is to go into my room, which is right next door. Instead of turning left, though, I turn right and go into the bathroom. I walk further into the bathroom and turn slowly around, taking in the details... the vinyl tile floor, the medicine cabinet that has mirrored doors, the pink brush with black bristles sitting on the left side of the counter.

I look quickly into the hallway across to my room. The door is closed, and I hear the sound of an old car pulling into the driveway. I look out the window. Someone has driven my stepfather to our house. I can feel my heart skip slightly. He and my mom are supposed to be separated. He isn't supposed to be here.

I am relieved because the front door is locked so we are safe, and I think about calling my mom at work. I turn around quickly, and he is standing right there: Cowboy boots, faded jeans, T-shirt tucked in, black leather belt with an eagle buckle.

The back door. I forgot he had a key. I swallow the panic, so second nature, but I am too quick to speak and say:

"You aren't supposed to be here."

He smiles a thin, quiet smile. I've shown my hand. He knows he caught me off guard.

My brother and sister come out of his room into the small hallway, smaller now with him here. My sister stands behind me. My stepfather picks up my brother. This is when I know that they have made up again. This is when I know that my mom didn't think telling me ahead of time was important...

So anyway, I take my brother from his arms and hand him to my sister, turning them towards my bedroom.

"It's time for bed," I tell him, "and I told them they could sleep with me."

My room is dark, but I push them in quickly and shut the door. I turn back to him and smile. I have a job to do now. The job is easy; keep them safe. As long as he is not alone, there is no reason for him to go looking for us. I hope he passes out quickly.

I swallow the rest of the panic and hug him. Stale Marlboro clings to his shirt. He smells sweet, stale: whiskey but not too much.

"Did you want a beer?" I say, walking past him, away from my siblings and down the stairs into the kitchen. He follows.

He goes to the fridge and pulls out a can, cracking the tab before shutting the door. He stumbles just a little as he heads down into the family room.

"Make some popcorn," he orders.

I wait as the oil heats in the pan. I am tired, so completely tired. I am on autopilot.

"Make sure I have two baloney sandwiches in my lunch this time, two slices each," he yells up the stairs. "Last time, there was only one."

I watch the popcorn pop.

"And put more than five chips in. I'm not a fat-ass like you," he says.

I fixate on the sound of popping corn.

"Did you hear me?" he says angrily.

I pull two glass bowls down out of the cupboard and set them on the counter next to a knife. One bowl is yellow, one red. I can hear him coming closer to the stairs.

"Did you fucking hear me?" he yells.

I ignore him, pouring popcorn back and forth into both bowls as he comes up the stairs. I pick up the red bowl that is overflowing with popcorn, holding it to my chest in my right arm. I pick up the knife with my left.

"Hey, I'm fucking talking to you," he yells, grabbing the arm with the popcorn.

He spins me around, and as I turn to face him, I shove the knife upward through the middle of his chest while my eyes meet his.

He gasps and pulls back. As he moves, I turn the knife so that as he pulls back it is harder to remove. It is harder to turn than I imagined it would be. There is blood on my hand. It is slippery, and I let go. He stumbles backwards into the counter and then lands on the floor. He tries to get up, reaching for the phone. With the bowl still cradled in my arm, I walk past him and up the stairs towards my room.

My sister has come to the door. I meet her there.

"Here," I say, handing her the bowl, "I thought you might want some."

"Won't we get in trouble?" she says.

"No, don't worry about it. Eat your popcorn and go to bed. I'll be up in a while," I tell her.

She shoves some popcorn in her mouth as she goes back into my room and I go back to the kitchen.

My stepfather has managed to pull the receiver down to the floor but cannot manage to get up to reach the dial. There is blood everywhere.

I walk around him, and he tries to reach out to grab my leg. I step to the side and around him, reach down and pull the knife out of his chest. His eyes are closed now. I wipe the knife off on his pants and put it on the counter. I pick up the yellow bowl of popcorn. I look at him as I put a handful of popcorn into my mouth, then walk past him, sit on the hallway stairs and listen to him struggle to get up.

I eat popcorn, one piece at a time, and wait for my mom to get home."

"So, what are you going to do with all of that rage?" LilyQ asked.

"You know exactly what I am going to do," Lex responded, hearing a knock on her front door.

"Someone's here, hold on, I'll be back..."

Lex opened the door to Detective Dixon.

"Yes?" she asked.

"I thought I would return these to you," he told her, holding out a box, "just sign this. Do you have family?" he asked.

"Yes. My son, my granddaughter, my daughter-in-law," Lex answered.

"Yes, but anyone else? Brothers, sisters?" he asked.

"Not that it should have anything to do with anything, but no. But you know that already. So, why ask?"

He sighed, answering:

"No reason."

"Well, I doubt that," she offered. "What do you want?"

He ignored the question, handing her the box.

"Here are your items. Unbroken as promised," he told her.

She took the box from him, commenting:

"We could have picked them up."

He stood silent.

"If you have something to say, then say it," she told him.

"Ok," he began, "I don't believe any of this."

Lex laughed, "Well, I would love to make your day, but I'm not that interesting."

He stood silent a moment, then offered, "Good luck to you then. Take care."

He turned to leave, then turned back and spoke:

"Whatever it is, walk away. You seem like a nice lady with a nice family. I'd hate to see you destroy them. Or yourself."

She watched him walk away, then opened the box.

True to his word, everything was in perfect condition. At the bottom of the box was his business card. She turned it over.

"If you decide to talk."

"Hmm," she said out loud and tossed the card in the trash.

One thing was for sure, she always learned from her mistakes. Confiding without anonymity was a big one. Detective Dixon was a nice man. She hoped he found other things to do while he waited to retire. What was it...two and a half years? She curled up on the sofa with a game controller and clicked 'X'. The character Avery decorated came up, and she laughed out loud at the sight of it.

'It' was purple with an oversized head, small arms, big hands and orange feet. The smile was hand drawn and was almost as high as the eyes on each side. The eyes, that were once green, were now brown, the only characteristic on the character that only she could change. The eyes always told the truth and were the reminder that this was indeed a real live person. It kept the world real.

"Ready to play?" it asked.

She clicked 'X' for yes.

Embedded in the screen, a smaller screen popped up. As her character hopped across a stream by jumping from one rock to the next, picture after picture appeared on the screen while the profiles of the real people appeared in several paragraphs. All from LilyQ. Her choice of who to take on next.

'*I'm going to find you,*' Lex thought of LilyQ as she flipped through the profiles.

She sighed.

Probably, one day, she would get caught. Her secrets would be exposed for everyone to judge. Aiden would know she betrayed him. Avery would know that Grandma made choices for her that could never be changed. Lex would lose everything that had any real importance.

Probably, she would end up in a small cell for what remained of her life. Or maybe an anxiety attack would actually be a heart attack. Dixon's words haunted her, and she knew he was right. She could stop. Or she couldn't. This was so automatic now. Compulsive.

She clicked back to the original screen and typed:

"I'm back. Miss me?"

Lex pictured herself sitting there on the stairs as a child, eating popcorn, blood sticky on her hands.

She remembered fighting the officers as she was dragged away.

She heard her mother's screams and saw the tears on her sister's face as her mother held her back, separating them forever.

She could still hear the echo of the heavy metal door being locked and she could feel the hot, heavy medication send her into unconsciousness.

Lex smiled. Probably all of this would get her killed. But not today.

'...I've drawn regret from the truth of a thousand lies, so let mercy come and wash away what I've done...' –Linkin Park

Epilogue

The young woman watched as the words popped up on her screen:

"I'm back. Miss me?"

She moved to respond but stopped when she heard him call to her:

"Hey, are you coming to bed?"

"In a few minutes babe. I'm finishing some work," she called back.

She began to type her reply, the White Rabbit tattoo glowing in the luminescence.

"Of course. Welcome back..."

Made in the USA
Las Vegas, NV
03 March 2022

44945338R00159